Special Offers

Book 1 of the Coursodon Dimension Series

M.L. RYAN

ISBN: 0615672760
ISBN-13: 978-0615672762

ACKNOWLEDGMENTS

Thanks to my test readers, Amy and Shary (LY,BNLM), and my editors for finding all the errors I managed to miss.

Special thanks to my husband and son, who showed remarkable patience while I undertook this endeavor and encouraged me to continue.

For my boys

CONTENTS

~Prologue~

Being without a body wasn't as unsettling as the enforcer imagined. He hadn't accounted for how much energy was consumed with the mundane, but entirely necessary, acts of keeping his body up and running. Now, free of the everyday physiological processes beyond anyone's control—breathing, heartbeat, cell division—he never felt more powerful and alive.

Not that he was dead. Not technically, at least. He'd spent decades searching for a way to preserve himself should one of the villainous reprobates he pursued manage to kill him. Possessing extraordinary magical prowess aided in this endeavor—if anyone could achieve such a feat, it would be him, of course.

I knew human technological innovation would prove invaluable. Kess, you are truly a genius.

Allowing himself the indulgence of a few extra moments of self-congratulatory veneration—it was well-deserved, after all—he focused on the next phase of the process. Though the magic rose with familiar ease, bending it to his will proved a more difficult challenge.

Long before exhausting himself with the effort, he recognized something had gone inexplicably and horribly wrong. As planned, his thoughts, memories, and dazzling personality—the parts responsible for making him so gloriously him—were no longer associated with his mortally damaged physical shell. They were, however, trapped, where he was not certain, but decidedly not in the place he intended.

There was no need to panic, he reminded himself. Throughout his long life, he had survived scores of perilous situations, all because he used his intellect and training to find a solution. This would be no different.

He merely required time and a bit of good fortune.

~1~

I f I had any inkling that my world would be irrevocably altered by a seemingly mundane purchase, I would have cut up my credit cards or sworn off the on-line shopping. But, like many things in life, you never realize at the time that one decision can change everything.

The day started as mine usually did, being jolted awake at six a.m. by the alarm clock set to my favorite oldies radio station. I smacked the off button just as a *The Presidents of the United States* song was ending and dragged myself out of bed with the lyrics, *Movin' to the country, gonna eat a lot of peaches*, lingering in my sleep-addled brain.

It was still completely dark outside. Not that it's unusual for January, but in Arizona, where for some reason we never switch to Daylight Savings Time, the sun wasn't going to rise for a while. There's something very disconcerting about waking before the sun. If God had wanted us to get up when it was still dark out, he wouldn't have given us eyelids.

I shuffled towards the kitchen, robotically starting a pot of much-needed coffee. The task was so ingrained I didn't remember measuring the grounds or filling the reservoir with water. Somehow, despite no coherent thought, each morning I managed to make a respectable brew. A good thing, too. Without adequate caffeination, everyone I came in contact with would be in grave peril.

As the aromatic deliciousness drifted through the compact kitchen, my cat wound himself around my ankles. He made an insistent *burr-ip* sound that roughly translated to, "Good morning, human, I'm so happy you're up. Now feed me, lazy tramp." To make me move faster, Vinnie repeatedly jammed his furry head into my ankles, which only served to thwart my attempts to open his bag of food.

"Hold on, you miserable beast. I'm still mostly asleep," I scolded, shaking some food into his bowl. It occurred to me that we did the same thing every morning: alarm, coffee, meowing, kibble. Well, except weekends. Then, the alarm could be eliminated, but the rest of the list stayed redundantly intact. How I managed the excitement was one of the universe's enduring mysteries.

The moment I finally set the bowl on the floor, Vinnie began to scarf down his breakfast with the utter abandon that only an eighteen-pound feline can muster. You'd think I starved him the way he dove into the stuff, but maybe setting world records for feline food guzzling was his way of compensating for being an anomaly in the animal world. When I picked him out from a litter of kittens being given away at the Swap Meet, I naturally assumed that he was a she as 99.99% of calicos are girls. I was particularly drawn to the triangular patches of color that extended over each eye, one black and one orange, that made him look like a pirate. It wasn't until the next day, when the vet revealed that the tri-colored kitty I'd named after a medieval Norwegian female swashbuckler was, in fact, male, that Alvida became Vinnie.

In truth, almost everything associated with me was out of the ordinary. Case in point: I had an extra lumbar vertebra in my back and my father was missing one. The fact that I had six instead of five and my dad only had four didn't make any difference to either of us physically, but it was bizarre. Maybe there's a familial quota for bones, and somewhere in the cosmic karma, my dad and I evened it out.

Then, there was my job. I got my master's degree in physiology and worked for a few years in a research laboratory at the University of Arizona. When the economy tanked, grant funding dried up and eventually my boss—a full professor—was arrested for pimping high-priced hookers. He had been using his ill-gotten gains to keep the research going, but despite his motivation, was now serving his sentence in a medium security prison outside of Winslow. After a brief period of wallowing in the despair of unemployment, I landed a fairly well-paying gig at a small, local artisan cheese factory. Not just any cheese, but that made from chinchilla. Unbeknownst to me, a previously untapped market for cheese made from the mammary secretions of animals other than goats or cows existed, and I was gifted with a talent for milking the small, furry creatures. Rich people will buy anything, apparently, particularly if it is unique and pricey.

When the coffee was ready, I poured a cup and looked around my current home, a *casita* on the grounds of a much larger, mostly vacant main house. Two people could barely fit into the kitchen at the same time, and while technically a one-bedroom, even a double-sized mattress left little space for anything else. The living room was accordingly miniscule, able to fit only a loveseat and a small table with two chairs. I added ceiling-high bookshelves along every available stretch of wall, each packed two or three deep with paperbacks.

"I really have to do something about these books," I said out loud. I loved fiction and kept every book I'd ever read. Not that I ever re-read most of them, but for some reason couldn't bring myself to get rid them, either. Unfortunately, there wasn't room for any more unless I moved to a bigger place, but the thought of packing up everything was too terrible to contemplate. Besides, the rent was reasonable and the location fantastic; it was close to everything but isolated enough to give the impression of being in the middle of nowhere.

Not wanting to waste any more still under-caffeinated brainpower on this dilemma, I set the half-empty cup next to my laptop and checked my email. The first one hawked penis enlargement—which I quickly deleted—the next was from my mother—which I ignored—and the last was sent from Amazon. Occasionally, I bought books online through Amazon, and figured this was probably a push to purchase some new best-seller based on my previous buying history. While preferring to visit bookstores to find new material, I had to admit having them shipped directly to my home was way more convenient.

The email was not what I expected, but an ad for their latest Kindle. I'd always balked at switching to an electronic book reader. First, they weren't cheap; I could buy a lot of books for the price of the reader itself. Second, the feel of the pages seemed an essential component to the reading experience, and last, but certainly not least, I worried that the widespread use of electronics would mean the end of brick-and-mortar bookstores. Still, the idea that one could have thousands of books in one thin device seemed like the answer to the problem of my ever-encroaching book collection.

My interest piqued, I noticed an option with "special offers." For a reduced price, advertisements—mostly for other books—would appear when the device was turned on. I scanned the fine print to reassure myself that, indeed, there weren't going to be ads popping up intermittently in the text. Still not completely convinced, I wasted a good fifteen minutes watching videos of cats being scared by cucumbers before revisiting the discounted Kindle concept. Another ten minutes later, I let out a long sigh of resignation, said "what the hell," and ordered the damned thing. Vinnie chose that moment to walk across the keyboard and arch his back, his way, I supposed, to let me know he thought I was a sellout.

"Hey, it was either this, or I'd have to put you on a diet to make more room in here," I snapped.

He turned his chubby body, lifted his tail—providing a much too up close and personal view of his butt—before leaping off the laptop and sauntering into the bedroom.

"Sure, everyone's a critic," I mumbled as I downed the last of the coffee.

~2~

The time spent online shopping meant if I didn't want to be late for work, I'd have to skip either my morning trail-run or straightening my long hair. It was a tough choice, but I opted to forgo the more energy-intensive undertaking. After completing the two-mile scamper through the desert, I showered and let my hair dry naturally into a somewhat contained mass of curly ringlets.

That accomplished, I pulled on my standard work attire—jeans and a t-shirt. That was the beauty of living in Tucson, anything other than denim was considered dressed up. At this time of year, it could be thirty-five degrees when I left for work, but seventy-five by the time I got home. As an accommodation to the seasonal temperature swing, I opted for long-sleeves from late November through March.

I glanced in the mirror, making a pre-departure Hailey-check. Of average height with an average build, people said I was pretty, and occasionally I did think I looked … not bad. Mostly, I considered myself to be fairly ordinary in the looks department. My dark brown hair never seemed to do exactly what I wanted it to, although the frizz factor was definitely diminished in Arizona's low humidity. Instead of exotically hued eyes of azure or emerald, mine were brown—and not even a lovely shade of cognac or amber, just … brown. I had decent skin, and didn't generally wear much makeup, except mascara, to accentuate my best feature—extremely long, thick eyelashes. Unfortunately, this attribute caused swooning only from other women, and therefore wasn't a big draw when it came to attracting members of the opposite sex. Not that I cared much about dating; my most recent boyfriends had all been characters in books. Resigned to my unremarkable looks and self-imposed relationship moratorium, I headed out to work.

It was only a fifteen-minute drive, and being the first one in, I started a pot of coffee and checked the schedule to see how many chinchilla were scheduled for milking.

About six months before, I was promoted to dairy manager, which meant my new duties involved mainly supervising a crew of five—three who worked during the week and two more who kept an eye on things over the weekend. Despite some people's objections to using chinchilla in such a way, the critters were treated like farm animals. Better, actually. Socialized from birth to get comfortable with the milking process, when their dairy days were over, all were offered for adoption to scrupulously pre-screened owners. Their expansive temperature and humidity controlled indoor area included access to a safety-screened outdoor enclosure when it wasn't too hot outside. We had free-range chinchilla.

I moved through the door to their play area, flipped on the lights, and opened the barriers from the nesting rooms so the little beasties could scamper in. About five or six were already nibbling on some manzanita branches by the time I lifted the last of the four metal panels that separated the areas. One of my favorites, Bessie, wandered over and rubbed against my foot. As I bent down to scratch under her soft, silvery neck, I heard a muffled voice call out, "Morning, Hailey".

Through the big glass window between the animal area and the office, was Rachel, depositing her lunch into the fridge on the far side of the room. Despite the fact that she was drop-dead gorgeous, she was my best friend and confidant. She had every physical feature I would have killed for—naturally straight, pale-yellow hair, expressive green eyes and full lips, all atop a shapely figure propped up by long, slender legs. Rachel was also unfailingly upbeat and the luckiest person I knew. She met her current boyfriend, Harrison, when she called the Pima County Fire Department to dispose of a rattlesnake that had coiled on her front porch. Four firemen promptly arrived, all young and hot, one of whom was Harrison. Sparks flew, romance ensued, and they'd been inseparable for months. That would never happen to me. I'd get the ready-for-retirement curmudgeon with indigestion from the firehouse chili. All of which should have provided ample grounds for jealous loathing, but I adored her nonetheless.

Rachel grabbed her *Support Your Right to Arm Bears* mug from atop the coffee maker, poured herself a cup, and spooned in her usual three heaping teaspoons of sugar. She gave it a couple of quick stirs and took a long sip.

Sighing with contentment, she leaned against the desk, and as I made my way into the office, asked, "You want some?"

"Sure," I responded, turning on my computer.

While I waited for it to boot up, I twisted my curls into a bun, securing the still slightly damp mess with some hair sticks to achieve my workday hairstyle. I loved using hair sticks; it was a fast, simple means to contain my often out-of-control hair, and it was more interesting than a ponytail. Basically, anything thin and pointy would suffice and sometimes, in a pinch, I resorted to using two pencils. Rachel liked to joke that I could use chopsticks, and then just yank them out of my hair when it was time to eat Chinese food. Harrison thought they could be useful in the unlikely event of a mugging.

Rachel handed me my mocha-java and proceeded to add yet another spoonful of sugar into her cup.

I grimaced at the concoction. "How can you ruin perfectly good coffee like that? Can you even taste anything other than cloying sweetness?"

"I don't know how you can stand to drink it black," she countered. "Besides, it's like having coffee and a doughnut all in one without the extra fat. It's really a very sensible diet strategy."

Before I could formulate a sarcastic retort, our other weekday co-workers swept in, arguing about which local eatery had the best margaritas.

"Casa Arvizu, definitely," pronounced Daniel as he set his water bottle on top of the fridge.

"Sure, if you define best as biggest. But quality-wise, no one can beat La Mariposa," Chelsea replied.

Chelsea and Daniel looked like they were brother and sister; both had short, straight, blue-black hair, gray eyes, and athletic builds. They were, however, not related, which was fortunate because they had been dating for the past three years and living together for two.

Setting the rectangular plastic container that she was holding on my desk, Chelsea dramatically peeled off the cover. "Ta da! Brownies!" she announced proudly.

I peered down at the pile of crumbly, grayish squares as Chelsea informed us that she used half-and-half instead of low-fat milk to make up for the butter required for the recipe that she didn't have. Chelsea was well known for never acquiring everything needed to properly complete a dish, meaning she often came up with interesting replacement ingredients to make up for the missing items, with variable results. She used the same culinary philosophy to pair seemingly unpairable foods into bizarre concoctions. I still hadn't completely recovered from the peanut butter and hummus sandwiches she brought for a pot luck lunch the year before.

Looking up, I smiled brightly. "What bad luck; I just had a big breakfast. I'll wait to have one after lunch." I turned to offer them to Daniel, but he was no longer in the room, craftily escaping to begin sweeping the nesting rooms.

Rachel, who was too nice to craft an excuse, snagged one and courageously took a bite. Chewing for a long time, she tried to swallow, but eventually was forced to gulp some coffee before she could speak. She managed a muffled, "Not bad," despite the remaining wad of Grayie that made it appear as if she was using her cheek for winter food storage. "A little dry, but once you get past that, the flavor is excellent."

Chelsea beamed at the non-critical review and left to start her own morning tasks. When she was finally out of sight, Rachel whirled and spit the rest into the garbage.

"Oh my God! I've had crackers that were moister," she complained, quickly downing the rest of her coffee. "Too bad they have chocolate in them or we could have ground them up and given them to the critters to roll around in instead of their usual dust baths."

Somehow, I managed to make it through the day without being forced to sample the baked goods or disparage Chelsea's well-intentioned misadventures in baking. When it was time to head home, Daniel and Chelsea were still engaged in margarita comparisons, having at least settled that frozen was better than on the rocks and *sin sal* was a sin.

I left them to their debate, climbed into my trusty RAV4, and drove through evening traffic. Once home, I made a quick assessment of my dinner options, which were limited to corn flakes or frozen burritos. I opted for a burrito because it only had to be microwaved while the cereal required the additional steps of getting a bowl and pouring in the milk.

When it was heated, I peeled back the plastic wrapper and ate it like a push-up pop while flipping through the TV channels. I stopped at ESPN and watched a couple of men's college basketball games until it seemed like a good time to go to sleep. I washed my face, brushed my teeth, changed into sleep shorts and camisole top, and then slipped into bed. Vinnie followed his usual nightly routine—burrowing under the covers and curling up near my feet. I sighed and flipped off the bedside lamp.

As I lay in the darkness, it occurred to me that I must be the most boring, single, thirty-year-old ever. I didn't go out much. I ate crappy food. I couldn't even remember the score of the games I just watched.

This was not how I had imagined myself at this point in my life. Had my marriage not crashed and burned, I'd probably have a baby by now. Yeah, and I would still be married to an asstard. He probably would have spawned asstardlets. I just wanted to feel like my life was going somewhere—like I was accomplishing *something*. I rolled onto my side and vowed to try to get myself together and move forward.

When I finally fell asleep, I dreamt I went on my first post-divorce date. The faceless guy took me to a fancy restaurant, ordered lots of food and expensive wine, and then ditched me for the voluptuous hostess. I was presented with the check, but lacked any means of paying it. After negotiating a payment plan with the restaurant owner—which involved allowing him to indulge his foot fetish with my pinkie toes and some flavored whipped cream—I left the place and got into my car, which was really weird because my date drove.

There in the parking lot were dine-and-dash and the hostess, groping each other with abandon. I revved up the engine, threw the car into drive, and peeled out towards them. The headlights illuminated their stunned faces as I spun the car sharply, rolled down the window, and chucked a lit Molotov cocktail—made from the empty wine bottle from dinner—at them and sped off humming the theme to *The Lion King*.

I woke up thinking I must be making progress. Usually in my dreams, I ran them over after I set them on fire.

~3~

The next day was Friday, and it was splendidly uneventful. As the workday wound down, everyone discussed their plans for the weekend: Chelsea and Daniel were driving up to the White Mountains to ski, and Rachel and Harrison were going to some new foreign film at The Loft, a local, independent movie theater near campus. I intended to do laundry and re-caulk the bathtub.

Rachel was particularly displeased with my plans, and spent the entire afternoon trying to coax me to come to with them.

"Come on, it'll be better than sitting around by yourself," she pleaded. "Maybe Harrison can get one of his co-workers to join us. It'll be fun."

"Fun?" I blurted. "A, the last foreign film you coerced me into seeing was so awful I was tempted to choke myself into unconsciousness to avoid having to subject myself to the torture of watching the second hour, and, B, I would rather be tied to a horse and dragged by my tongue than get fixed up."

"No need to be snotty," Rachel answered, scowling. "I'm just worried that you spend too much time alone."

I wrapped my arms around her and gave her a quick hug. "I appreciate the concern. I really do. I'm just not ready for another relationship yet. Or, to wake myself from a French-ciné-induced coma," I added with a grin.

"Who's talking about a relationship?" she argued, pulling away. "I was thinking more in terms of one date. When was the last time you had one?"

Her accusatory tone stung, but I knew she had a point. I hadn't been on a date since my divorce, and that had been almost three years. Rachel seemed to recognize the harshness of her tone, because she turned to face me and placed her hands on my shoulders.

"Hey, I'm sorry. I'm worried about you and just want you to be happy. Promise you'll call me if you want to get together and do something Saturday or Sunday, okay?"

I assured her that if I came up with anything interesting, she would be the first to know. As Rachel headed out, I left some notes for the weekend guys and made certain none of the chinchilla had eluded the end-of-day roundup into the nesting area. Satisfied that everyone was where they should be, I flipped off the lights in the office and locked the doors.

Remembering to stop at the grocery store for needed provisions, I packed my cart with fresh veggies and fruit, avoiding the frozen food section completely. I also grabbed a pre-roasted chicken, a loaf of freshly-baked, whole-wheat bread, and a dark chocolate bar. Hey, you can't change old habits all at once.

When I got home, I noticed a package on the doorstep. I put all the groceries away and went back to pick it up, realizing it was the Kindle I ordered the morning before. *Gotta love that one-day shipping*, I thought, opening the box. Skimming through the instructions, I plugged it in to charge while I fixed dinner. Well, I made a salad and yanked some meat off the chicken—but compared to my usual fare, it was a huge improvement. I ate, cleaned up and carefully read how to set up the eBook reader. Once the light at the bottom indicated a full charge, I configured everything for my Wi-Fi and fired it up.

The advertisements were, as advertised, not particularly egregious, but I had some trouble navigating the Kindle Store on the device, deciding instead to search for reading material on my laptop. I decided to get one of the many classic books that can be downloaded free as my first purchase-not-purchase. I chose *Pride and Prejudice* by Jane Austen, and directed it to *Hailey's Kindle*. Moving to said device, I pushed the menu button, clicked *turn wireless on*, and then *sync and check for new items*.

Right before *Download Complete* appeared in the top left corner, I felt an odd, tingly sensation in my fingertips that then traveled up my arm, through my torso, and down to my toes. With the winter relative humidity hovering around 10%, I chalked up the occurrence to static electricity, glanced back to the Kindle, and sure enough, there was P & P!

I curled up on the sofa and began reading, pleased that what was on the screen looked just like the page of a book. About halfway through the first chapter, I laughed out loud when, instead of clicking the button, I moved my hand to flip the nonexistent page. An hour or so later, while I'd mastered the proper way to advance the text, could barely keep my eyes open. Much as I wanted to continue, the adventures of Lizzie and Mr. Darcy would have to wait until tomorrow. I put the Kindle to sleep and set about to do the same with myself.

When I awoke the next morning, sunlight was already leaking out around the edges of the mini-blinds in my room. I hadn't slept well, and while I couldn't quite remember all the details, I knew along with tossing and turning, I had some weird, intense dreams. Even for me. I glanced at the clock on my nightstand, it read eleven-fifteen. *Shit, I hope I'm not catching something,* I grumbled silently, dragging myself out of bed. I felt a little off, but didn't have a scratchy throat or runny nose, my usual harbingers of an oncoming cold. Whatever the problem, I decided to take it easy, and popped a couple zinc tablets to try to fend off any virulent microbe that might be multiplying inside me.

I made coffee and instant oatmeal, and listened to *Car Talk* while I ate. I knew nothing beyond the make and model of my own car, but the Magliozzi brothers made the inner workings of the combustion engine entertaining—whether you were into auto repair or not. When the show ended, I got dressed and decided to relax outside on the patio while I continued with *Pride and Prejudice*. The temperature was mild—close to seventy degrees—and I settled into the padded, zero-gravity chaise with the Kindle. I planned to read, but once nestled in the lounger, closed my eyes and listened to the low, raspy song of a cactus wren instead.

Cactus wrens are spunky birds that protect their large, elaborate nests by constructing them in the thorny branches of cholla cactus, a shrub-like plant with cylindrical stems made up of numerous, small, segmented pods. When brushed against, the thorns jam into your flesh, forcing the pods to release from the cactus. Which hurts like hell, by the way. A fine-toothed comb is the best means to remove them without the added ignominy of impaling your fingers, but predators generally don't have the foresight to carry such implements with them while raiding nests. Instead, they tend to try to remove the stickers using their mouths, which also must hurt like hell. All told, the cactus provided a fine security system for the wren nestlings.

The next thing I knew, the sun was low in the western sky. *Fuck*. I'd just slept another four hours, at least. *I must be getting something*. Stiff from lying in one position for so long, I still didn't feel ill exactly. Just … strange. Probably from too *much* sleep, I reasoned.

Gingerly rising to my feet, I stretched, and went inside. The clock on the microwave proved what I'd expected, it was almost five, and I'd wasted a perfectly good Saturday. My stomach rumbled, reminding me my last meal was the oatmeal hours before, and oddly, I had a taste for beef. Not that I was a vegetarian, but I usually only ate chicken or fish. Every so often, however, I had a hankering for a big, juicy sirloin, and this, apparently, was one of those rare—or, my preference, medium—occasions. Probably had something to do with my funk of undetermined origin.

I didn't really want to go out, either to a restaurant or to the store to buy a steak, and settled on ordering from a local joint that delivered. Their foot-long Italian beef sandwich managed to assuage my red meat cravings and the added green peppers and onions made me feel like I was keeping to my quest for a healthier diet.

Feeling a bit more energetic after the meal, I tackled some much-needed laundry. While the second load was in the dryer, I read a few more chapters (38% completed!) before I again grew weary.

"Whatever this is, I hope it gets out of my system soon," I complained to Vinnie, who was asleep, curled up on the clean clothes folded in the laundry basket. He looked up and yawned when I spoke, then stood, reversed his position, nestled into the garments, and promptly dozed off again. If I wanted sympathy, I certainly wasn't going to get any from a creature that normally slept twenty hours a day. I picked up the basket with him still inside and moved into the bedroom. Which took some effort— the cat weighed a ton.

"Sorry, beast," I said as I gently prodded him to move. "You have to get out."

As I reached beneath him for a clean camisole and sleeping shorts, Vinnie begrudgingly hopped out onto the bed. He spent a few moments in the decidedly catty endeavor of nonchalantly licking his front paw to indicate the insignificance of being booted from his comfortable spot.

Ignoring his feline melodrama, I brushed my teeth and changed, then tucked myself into bed, holding up the sheet so Vinnie could assume his usual spot at my feet. As he settled, I felt another odd, mild jolt, this time just in my torso. It lasted only a fraction of a second, but Vinnie hissed, shot out from under the covers, ran over my chest and out of the room. Confused at the bizarre behavior, I stared at the door, waiting for him to return. When he didn't, I went into the living room, turned on the light, and found him cowering near the front door.

"Here, sweet boy," I cooed as I crouched down, extending my hands in what should have been a reassuring gesture. To my dismay, he hissed again, and ran under the TV stand. I stood there for a minute, absorbing the sting of his rebuff, before reluctantly returning to bed.

Staring into the dark, I tried to make sense of what had happened. Vinnie had never acted that way toward me before. *Maybe he heard a coyote outside and that freaked him out,* I rationalized. It wasn't unusual for coyotes, or even javelina—a type of wild, skinny pig-like creature—to hang around outside. In fact, a javelina family took up nightly residence on my front porch a couple of weeks before. Vinnie had been agitated at their presence, and spent a lot of time peering out the window at the group, but he never acted like he was possessed.

"Great, I feel like crap and am rejected by my own pet," I murmured, as sleep finally overtook me.

***

The next morning, I felt more like myself. Sleeping for almost an entire day must have taken care of whatever ailed me and Vinnie's disposition had improved as well. He was still avoiding me, but at least he stopped hissing.

Making use of the new-found energy, I took a morning hike on the Ventana Canyon Trail, and afterward, treated myself to lunch at In-N-Out Burger. I hadn't eaten a double-double for the longest time, but for some reason, I just had to have one. Or two, as it turned out.

In the afternoon, I'd started paying some bills when my cell phone rang. *Probably Rachel,* I thought as I stood to extract it. Surprisingly, it wasn't in its usual spot—wedged in the front pocket of my jeans—but on the kitchen counter. I glanced at the screen. It wasn't Rachel. In fact, I didn't recognize the number and it wasn't a local area code. Still, I answered it. What if Publisher's Clearing House was calling?

My "hello" was followed by silence, and then a rich, baritone voice on the other end said, "I'm returning your call. You must have hung up just before I had a chance to answer."

"You have the wrong number. I haven't called anyone," I responded politely. *Just my luck, no million-dollar winnings today.*

"I don't think so," he countered. "I used return missed call."

"I don't know what to tell you; it wasn't me."

"No one else might have used your phone?"

I was beginning to tire of the conversation, and regretted I hadn't ignored the call. "No, no one else used my phone." I spoke slowly, thinking it might be more comprehensible that way. "You have the wrong number. Bye now."

I hit the end button, jammed the phone into my pocket, and went back to the bills. About a half hour later, I was interrupted mid-online payment by more ringing. Transfixed by the amount of electricity I apparently used last month, I answered the phone without looking to see who it was.

"You called me again."

I looked at the number on the screen, and sure enough, it was Wrong Number Guy. I tried to remain courteous, but my exasperation crept out despite my good intentions.

"No, I did not. I don't know what your deal is, but it wasn't me."

"Well, someone did."

"There isn't anyone else here," I responded testily. "Something must be wrong with your phone."

After a pause, he said, "I'll look into that. Sorry to have disturbed you."

I didn't bother to say goodbye. Tossing the phone next to my laptop, I went back to my bills. Ironically, I was just finishing up the one from Verizon when the phone rang again.

I stared daggers at the now familiar number on the screen and quickly snatched it off the desk. Before I could release the litany of rants forming in my brain, Wrong Number Guy spewed forth a few of his own.

"Look, toots, I suppose you think it is amusing to keep phoning me and hanging up, but I find it annoying and extraordinarily rude. What are you, twelve years old or something?" he fumed. Your parents must be very proud."

"Toots?" I spat back. "What are you, one hundred and twelve or something? I told you twice already, I'm not screwing with you. I AM NOT CALLING YOU! I don't know why you think I am, but I'm not."

I continued describing what he could do with his obviously malfunctioning cellular device when he interrupted my tirade.

"What did you just say?"

He didn't sound angry—just confused. Truthfully, I couldn't remember exactly what I said. Trying to recall what may have caused his seemingly odd reaction, I thought I could buy myself some time by hedging with a feeble, but honest, "I have no idea what you are talking about."

"Yes, you do. You said, 'Sebastian'."

Now it all made sense. "I probably called you 'bastard' and you couldn't hear correctly because of your piece-of-shit phone."

"No, you said Sebastian," he insisted. "There were clearly three syllables."

Sebastian—a bastard—who cared?

"Whatever. I haven't been calling you. Stop calling *me* and leave me alone!"

I vaguely heard him saying something else as I ended the call, but at that point, I was more than ready to be done with him.

"What an asshole," I said aloud, dropping the phone on the couch. I stared at it for a moment, then went over, picked it up, and turned off the ringer.

***

Given my practically comatose Saturday, the work week came way too soon. Monday morning, Vinnie was AWOL. After frantically searching, I finally found him cringing under my bed. Only food enticed him to come out, but when finished, he hid behind the shower curtain.

Maybe he's sick, I worried. He seemed to be eating okay, though it wouldn't be surprising if no matter what the malady, diminished eating would be the last symptom to emerge. I made certain that the hummingbird feeder hanging outside the front window was filled with sugar water to entertain him while I was gone. He could sit and stare at those pugnacious little birds for hours, moving only slightly during the staccato, mouth-twitching thing that cats do when they see prey.

It was my week to replenish the coffee accoutrements at work, and I stopped at the store on my way in. By the time I pulled into the parking lot at the farm, Rachel's car was already there. The nicest part of not arriving first was the heavenly scent of brewing java that hit me as I opened the front door. I took a deep breath of the heady bouquet and deposited the new container of half-and-half in the fridge.

"Wow, that smells great," I remarked to Rachel, who had just come in from the playroom. "What is that?"

"A free sample I got at that new shop on Campbell. Some proprietary blend. I haven't had a chance to try it yet, but if it tastes as good as it smells, it should be fantastic."

I poured myself a cup and proceeded to get the morning chinchilla report from Rachel. The weekend crew hadn't properly secured one of the barriers and the critters had free reign in the playroom all night. I was about to tell her that I would help clean up the resultant mess when I noticed she was staring at me, her perfect brows furrowed.

I glanced down at my shirt, but saw no egregious stains that would elicit such a critical expression. "What's the problem?"

"Since when do you drink your coffee anything but black?" she asked.

I looked into my cup, surprised that its contents were a light toffee color. Further scrutiny revealed that the half-and-half container I'd just placed in the refrigerator was sitting on top of the table, and was open.

"Huh. I didn't even realize I'd added that," I shrugged as I put the carton back in the fridge. Actually, I didn't remember taking it out, either.

"You put in two teaspoons of sugar, too," she continued, her eyebrows now arched as if to say, "what gives?"

"Really?" I sniffed the contents of the cup before I took a tentative sip. I fully expected to be appalled by the concoction, but figured I'd try it rather than just dumping it down the sink.

Amazingly, the creamy, sweet mix wasn't completely terrible. In fact, it was bordering on delicious, but after years of poking fun at Rachel's habit of "tainting" her coffee, I held my tongue. Of course, when I quickly downed the whole thing and fixed another cup, my perfidy was pretty much exposed.

"Maybe you're pregnant," Rachel joked.

"Who's pregnant?" two voices called out simultaneously from the front entrance.

"Hailey," Rachel replied.

Chelsea and Daniel, who managed to catch only the last part of our conversation, appeared unfazed by the pronouncement. "Don't you have to have sex to get pregnant?" Daniel queried.

"So I've been told," I snapped back.

"Hailey just knowingly drank coffee with cream *and* sugar," Rachel proclaimed, clutching her chest in mock horror.

Smiling, Chelsea pointed out that the other likely explanation was that it could be a sign of the impending apocalypse.

"I thought the Cubs winning the pennant is the sign of the impending apocalypse," Daniel piped up.

"Very funny. You think my beverage choice is weird, yesterday I spent three hours watching Rugby on ESPN2."

That was, indeed, odd. I liked watching all kinds of sports on TV, but rugby was definitely not one of them. Even after the previous afternoon's scrumathon, I still wasn't sure about the rules, but found it strangely enjoyable. I had even searched for more matches to watch after the Wigan Warriors beat the Leeds Rhinos.

Rachel shook her head and laughed. "It could have been worse, it could have been NASCAR."

~4~

The rest of the week was pretty standard, but I still wasn't quite myself. Maybe I was still getting over my twenty-four hour bug from the weekend, or maybe all the added sugar I was now downing in my coffee was affecting my insulin levels.

On Friday morning, I got ready for a much-needed run. I'm not one of those people that leap out of bed in the morning ready to roll, but somehow, getting in a little jog first thing kind of gets me going. Besides, the way I had been feeling lately, maybe this would help shake off the cobwebs.

No need to assess the weather—I could see the sun was out and at this time of year in the Old Pueblo, I knew it would be chilly. I secured my hair into a ponytail atop my head, pulled on my running gear, and added a sweatshirt to counter the bite of the morning air. A few perfunctory stretches later, I began a slow but steady pace out of my neighborhood and down to the nearby River Park jogging trail.

I'm always amused that what the local powers-that-be call a river park is actually a paved pathway along the side of a bone-dry gulley. Occasionally, after a heavy rain (or three), the wash, as we call it, actually has a lot of water in it for a few hours and people flock to its edges to gawk at the flowing torrent as if they've never seen water before.

I was about halfway through my route when I noticed a man jogging toward me. I was accustomed to seeing the usual suspects during my runs. I guess most people have a routine that they like to stick to. There was the woman with long hair past her butt, who rode a bicycle while her Afghan hound lumbered alongside. The shirtless old dude who—regardless of the weather—never wore anything but running shorts and those weird, slipper-like shoes with space for each toe. Then there was the couple that walked a spotted dog, whose right ear was floppy, but the left one stood up straight. But this guy was someone I had never noticed before.

He was still at least a hundred feet in front of me, but even at that distance, I could tell he was tall and incredibly fit. He ran like he could go forever without breaking a good sweat. Bastard.

It wasn't long before our paths crossed and as they did, we gave each other the obligatory small nod that joggers give in greeting. I was right about the general lack of perspiration. All he had was the slightest glow of moisture on his forehead.

About ten feet further down the path, I tripped. I'm not sure on what, but then again, I wasn't really paying attention to where my feet were landing while I mentally dissed No Sweat Bastard. I tried to prevent the inevitable fall, but only managed to look even clumsier as I ended up wind- milling my flailing arms before landing on my knees. My now skinned flesh was encrusted with bits of gravel and hurt like hell.

"Son of a bitch," I groaned, as I rolled onto my side.

"Are you okay?" someone asked as they jogged up from behind. "You took quite a tumble."

I looked up into the bluest eyes I had ever seen. Who the hell has cornflower blue eyes? Great. He doesn't sweat while exercising and he has freakishly gorgeous eyes. And he just got to witness me take a header into the macadam.

"I'm fine. Just skinned up and massively embarrassed. I must have looked ridiculous."

"Not at all," he countered as he offered me a hand up. "Well, actually, I didn't really see anything as you were behind me. I heard you, but by the time I turned around, you were already down."

I declined the help, stood up, and dusted myself off. Close up, I now realized how tall he really was. He had to be at least six-five and I had to step back a bit to be able to look him in the face without craning my neck. His golden blonde hair was medium length, styled back from his face, and was sun streaked with almost silvery highlights. Not perfect features by any means; his nose looked like it might have been broken at some point—not exactly crooked, but a bit flattened toward the bridge and he had a thin, barely visible scar from bottom of his left nostril down to the top of his upper lip. All in all, he looked… nice.

"Are you sure you're alright? You're kind of oozing," he mused as he surveyed the damage to my knees.

Looking up from my tattered skin, he smiled broadly. Don't get me wrong, he was a good-looking guy. When he smiled, his whole face lit up and was transformed into something glorious.

"Uh, yeah, I guess I'd better get home and clean these off. Thanks for stopping."

"No problem. Do you run here a lot?"

"I live nearby, so this is one of my go-to morning jogs. Do you live around here?"

Oh god, could I be more lame? Do you live around here? Shit. I sounded like I'm in junior high.

"No, I'm here temporarily. I'm staying at a hotel about three miles from here. I figured I would go up to the bridge ahead and turn around," he said, gesturing toward the bridge about a quarter mile further along the path. "Maybe I'll see you again sometime."

He gave me another one of those dazzling smiles and jogged off. I watched him for a few seconds as he continued on his way. He had a nice body too—lean, but well-muscled. For an instant, I contemplated following him or waiting where I was until he came back this way.

"You really are pathetic," I said out loud.

I managed to hobble home without incident. Once I washed the crud off, the damage wasn't too bad. I showered and slapped a couple of giant, adhesive bandages on the worst parts and got ready for work.

Vinnie watched me dry my hair while sitting on the edge of the bathtub. He still wouldn't sleep in the bed with me, but for the most part his personality disorder from earlier in the week had abated. He padded over and weaved around my ankles as I grabbed my purse. I patted his furry head before I headed out.

By the time I got to the farm, I had only thought about No Sweat Bastard five or six times. Jeez. I really needed to get laid. It had been… a long time. A long, long time, in fact. Come to think of it, I hadn't come, to think of it, since an ill-advised one night stand with a co-worker at my last job right after my divorce was final. Damn. Had it really been almost three years? As I got out of my car, I vowed that I needed to at least attempt to get back in the game.

"Rachel, you know lots of people," I began while we were standing side by side in front of the coolers recording the day's milk production. It's always less difficult to have an uncomfortable conversation with someone when you are engaged in some other activity. "You don't happen to know any nice, single, uncomplicated guys, do you?"

An initial flash of surprise gave way to a relieved grin. "Thank god! Are you actually ready to date again?"

I paused, contemplating the implications of actually going out on a date after all this time. "Well, maybe I'm ready to think about dating anyway."

29

"Okay, not really the breakthrough we've all been waiting for, but it's a step in the right direction," she noted with a slight air of resignation.

"What do you mean 'we've all been waiting for'?" I asked suspiciously. "Is this something you all discuss a lot?" I frowned at the thought of people I knew and liked ruminating over my apparently gossip-worthy lack of a love life.

"Hey, we just worry about you. We want you to be happy."

"I'd be happier if you all weren't obsessing over my dating habits," I explained.

Rachel placed the final container of milk into the rack in the cooler before turning to face me.

"We aren't obsessing over your dating habits. We are obsessing over your *lack* of dating habits." With that comment, she moved past me and into the office.

"Sure, easy for you to say, she who makes men stop and stare when she walks by," I called out to her back. Now I was just getting snippy. I followed her, sulking, and plunked myself into my chair.

Rachel narrowed her eyes and pointed an accusatory finger in my direction. "Look, you are beautiful, but you might as well have a sign on you that says 'Back off!' If men aren't falling all over you, it's only because at some level, you don't want them to."

I knew she was right. Well, at least about the sign thing.

"I said I would think about dating," I uttered sheepishly. "I was thinking we should all try and meet at O'Reilly's tonight," I began as a means to change the topic. O'Reilly's was a pub far enough from the university campus to discourage the college crowd and centrally located enough for me, Rachel, Harrison, Chelsea, and Daniel not to have to drive all night to get there. The drinks were generous, they had tasty food specials, and a live band on Friday nights.

"Only if you let me scope out some potential man flesh for you while we're there," Rachel teased.

"Perfect," I replied. "But make sure he's rich, handsome, and intelligent."

"I thought you just wanted single, nice, and uncomplicated?" she countered.

"Well, since I'm so freaking hot, I decided to raise my standards."

***

It turned out that Chelsea and Daniel had already made other plans so it was just going to be Rachel, Harrison, and me. We planned to meet up around nine, but for some reason I was feeling antsy and I got there about a half hour early. I generally don't like sitting at the bar by myself, but it was already crowded and there weren't any empty tables. It looked like the band was getting ready to start a set, so I took a seat as far away from the stage as possible.

The bartender, Wyatt, a muscular, dreadlocked, redhead with colorful tattoos covering almost every inch of visible flesh, gave me a small wave as both greeting and indication that he was busy and would be with me shortly. Wyatt had been the regular bartender at O'Reilly's for as long as I had been going there. He mixed fine drinks, was usually pleasant, and didn't like to make small talk. If not for the fact that he was married and a rabid Arizona State fan, he might have been the perfect guy for me.

While I waited for Wyatt to take my order, I swung around on the stool and glanced about the room, searching for anyone I might know so I could hang with them instead of at the bar. No such luck. Someone slipped into the empty seat next to me and, from over my right shoulder, I heard "Hey, how's the knees?"

I turned back and was caught in the cornflower blue gaze of No Sweat Bastard. And he looked even better in the tight black t-shirt and black jeans he was wearing than he did this morning. The outfit accentuated his sinewy, athletic physique, while giving him a look of confident masculinity. Yum.

"I almost didn't recognize you with your hair down," NSB remarked. "It looks good this way."

As my bad luck would have it, Wyatt picked that moment to come by and ask what we wanted.

"You having your usual?" Wyatt drawled as he started to grab a bottle of Patron.

Wyatt knew me well. The only alcohol I ever drank was tequila—in either a margarita or straight. I heard someone say "No. Glen Fiddich, rocks," and realized that it was me.

I wanted to immediately right the obvious wrong that was my drink order, but I was too embarrassed to admit I had ordered misordered in front of NSB. I thought I noticed a flash of unease on his face when I asked for the scotch, but it was gone as soon as it appeared. He probably thought I was trying to seem exotic or something, ordering single-malt. Great, I fretted—now I was doubly self-conscious.

"I'll have the same," he directed toward Wyatt. To me, he said, "I never introduced myself this morning. I'm Alex. Alex Sunderland."

"Hailey Parrish," I replied. Not wanting the conversation to stall, the only thing I could come up with next was, "Wow. What are the odds that we would run into each other twice in one day?"

He unleashed one of those spectacular smiles my way and said, laughing, "Astronomical, I would think."

Just then, my purse started to vibrate. When I went out some place crowded, I liked to use one of those little cross-body bags instead of the behemoth I usually carried. That way, I was forced to limit myself to the essentials— phone, driver's license, lip-gloss, some cash, and a credit card—and I never had to worry about misplacing it in the throng. I excused myself, and turned away slightly as I grabbed the phone. It was Rachel.

"Hailey, I'm really sorry, but Harrison has some sort of stomach bug and he's currently curled in the fetal position on the bathroom floor moaning, 'kill me', over and over."

Ew. "That sounds awful. Does he need to go to urgent care?"

"No," she continued, "but you know men; they're such babies when they are sick. Obviously, we are going to have to beg off tonight. Are you already at the bar?"

"Yeah, I got here early," I yelled. Even with my finger pressed into my other ear, I could barely make out what she was saying with all the raucous bar noise. "Too bad Harrison's sick. Tell him I hope he feels better."

"I'm sure he will be by tomorrow. But I feel terrible that you are there by yourself."

"No problem," I assured her. *No problem, indeed*, I thought as I glanced at Alex, who was paying for both the drinks that Wyatt had just delivered. "Hey, it's really noisy in here, so I'm having a hard time hearing you. I'm fine, though. I'll just talk to you tomorrow."

I ended the call and set the phone on the bar. I wasn't particularly unhappy that they weren't coming. After all, Alex was easy on the eyes and Rachel would be so proud of me for talking to him instead of making an excuse to hide in the ladies' room. Besides, there was something about him that felt very familiar, like I had known him for a long time. Astounding as it seemed, I actually felt comfortable sitting with him.

As I turned to face him, he raised his glass towards me and I did the same with mine. We saluted each other with scotch and I took a sip. *God, this stuff really is wretched*, I thought, but somehow I felt compelled to keep drinking. And not just to keep up the pretense of having ordered something I actually liked. It was the weirdest feeling— wanting to both spit it out yet, at the same time, longing for the next mouthful. It occurred to me that maybe that's how all scotch drinkers feel. Because truly, the stuff tasted like turpentine.

Throughout the evening, the conversation encompassed the usual get-to-know you banter. I got the important information without too much digging; he was single and an insurance adjuster from Portland, Oregon in town for two weeks for some specialized training. He seemed sincere, but really, he could be from Salt Lake City and unemployed with ten kids for all I really knew. Not wanting to get into a complicated dialogue about my unusual career path, I just said I worked at a local dairy. That was my go-to angle when I wasn't in the mood to get into the specifics.

We ordered another round, which I paid for, and then switched to non-alcoholic choices—ice tea for me, sparkling water for him. He had a relaxed way about him that belied his obvious intellect and he shifted effortlessly between topics ranging from popular culture to global economies.

Too bad he doesn't live around here, I lamented. It figured that I meet a guy that I might actually like, and he's only here for two weeks. *No sense letting this go much further*, I reasoned. I certainly wasn't up for a one-nighter, or even, best-case scenario, a fourteen-nighter.

It was getting late, it had been a long day, and I wanted to drive home soon—before I risked falling asleep at the wheel. I rooted in my bag and found some bills to leave on the bar for Wyatt's well-deserved tip. Then I downed the last of my tea and turned to look at Alex.

"This has been fun," I began, "but I really should be getting home. Hope your training goes well. Maybe we'll run into each other again at the River Park."

As I started to get off the bar stool, a peculiar sensation coursed through me, as if I was suddenly exerting a great deal of energy. My expression must have communicated the discomfort, because Alex frowned and asked if I was okay. When I didn't immediately respond, he reached over and took my hands in his, concern etched across his handsome face.

Suddenly, I felt an electrical zap—similar to what I had encountered days before—when first synching the Kindle. I might have been able to rationalize it as some hackneyed romantic sign had the next two events not occurred in rapid succession. First, I inexplicably uttered one long, unrecognizable sound…then I heard the voice.

I always wondered how Kevin Costner's character in *Field of Dreams* managed to stay relatively calm when he first heard *"If you build it, he will come"* whispered in his cornfield. That was a movie, after all. When, in my head, a man uttered, "*I need his help*" repeatedly, I panicked. I tore myself from Alex's grip and ran through the crowded dance floor, shoving unsuspecting patrons out of my way as I quickly escaped out the emergency exit.

I sprinted to my car and managed to fish my keys out of my purse, despite the fact I was shaking from head to toe. Thankfully, the repetitive pleading of my auditory hallucination had ceased by then. I'm not really sure how I got home. I know I drove, but beyond that, I had no recollection of the journey. When I reached the safety of my house, I rushed inside and collapsed on the living room floor.

I had a cousin who heard voices. Well, actually she thought her stuffed animals were talking to her. By the time she was sixteen or so, she was no longer capable of coherent thought and was hospitalized for almost a year.

When she was discharged, the medications she was given stopped the banter in her mind, but she always seemed a little… muted. It was like she couldn't experience any extreme emotions anymore—good or bad. My family was not in the habit of talking about such uncomfortable topics, so her "ailment" was never discussed, except for an occasional whisper, and especially not with us kids. Which, I suppose, made the whole idea even scarier than if it was dealt with openly.

With my arms wrapped around my knees and tears streaming down my cheeks, I rocked back and forth in anguish, trying to convince myself that the same thing wasn't happening to me.

Not long after, the front door creaked slowly open. I didn't want to lift my head from its protective perch on my knees, but apparently, even insanity couldn't hinder my curiosity. It was Alex, the doorknob in one hand and my cell phone in the other, peering at me from the partially opened door.

"You ran out so fast that you forgot your phone," he said quietly. "You drove off before I could catch up to you, and I was worried, so I followed you."

He set the phone on a small table and proceeded to cross the short distance between us to crouch beside me. I turned my head away as he placed a comforting hand on my shoulder.

"Hailey, what happened back there?"

I wiped away some of the tears using my sleeve and contemplated the pros and cons of admitting to an almost complete stranger that I was probably crazy. Considering the likelihood that Alex already thought I was nuts, I decided I had nothing to lose by confiding in him.

"I don't know," I finally squeaked out. "I... I'm hearing voices or something. I think I'm going crazy."

"What kind of voices?" he calmly inquired.

Wow. He was really taking this well. You'd think his response would be more along the lines of running screaming out of my house, thankful that we hadn't had the chance to exchange numbers. Or bodily fluids.

"Well, not voices. A voice. A man's voice said, '*I need his help*.'"

Alex was silent for a moment, as if he was trying to find the right words. When he finally spoke, he said, "Hailey, look at me."

Reluctantly, I looked up. Alex gently placed his hands on either side of my face, forcing me to gaze into those mesmerizing eyes. His lips curved into a small, reassuring smile and he stated resolutely, "You are not crazy."

I wanted to believe him. He sounded so sure of himself. "And you know this based on your experience with insurance adjustment," I joked feebly, trying to lighten the mood as much as possible, considering the circumstances.

"No, I know that based on my experience with spiritual convergence."

~5~

I wasn't certain that I had heard him correctly, mostly because whatever he just said didn't make any sense. Of course, I could be a raving lunatic, which could also explain my lack of comprehension.

"Spiritual what?" I asked. God, I hoped he wasn't involved with some weird religious cult.

Alex stood and helped me to my feet. "Maybe we should get more comfortable," he said as he directed me towards the couch. "This could take a while."

I tucked myself into the throw cushions at one corner of the loveseat while Alex moved one of the chairs so that he could sit directly in front of me. He let out a long sigh and ran a hand through his already tousled hair.

"This is going to sound like an odd question, but, have you purchased any electronic devices lately? A new cell phone or a computer?"

He was right, that was an odd question. Maybe he wasn't a religious zealot, maybe he worked on commission at Best Buy. Given the circumstances, I was in no position to judge. When nothing came immediately to mind, I started to shake my head. Until I caught a glimpse of the Kindle resting on the bookshelf closest to where I sat.

"I bought this," I confessed, grabbing the reader, and holding it aloft. He took it from me and turned it over a couple of times. "I thought maybe it wasn't working right," I continued. "I got a pretty big shock when I first synched it."

"Like the jolt you felt in the bar tonight?"

I was momentarily speechless, a condition I didn't often experience. "You could feel that?" I murmured. *I thought it was just me.*

"Oh yes." He smiled ruefully. "Hailey, I wasn't completely honest with you earlier. I'm not an insurance adjuster. I'm... sort of a private investigator."

At least he wasn't trying to convert me or sell me something. "I knew you were too good looking to be in insurance."

He lasered me with a reproachful glare.

"Hey, when I get nervous, the smart-ass just comes cascading out of my mouth," I shrugged. "It's a character flaw. Get over it." Not intending to be so snippy, I added, "Uh, sorry. Please, go on."

His glare softened to cautious regard, but he continued. "A few days ago, I received a series of calls from an unknown number from this area code. Each time, the caller disconnected before I could answer. I assumed it was some kid playing some prank, but it became rather bothersome. So, I called the number back in an attempt to end the irritation."

My eyes grew wide. "You're the assho—uh, the guy from the phone?" I quickly corrected.

"Yes. I'm the asshole," he confirmed.

This was awkward. "Look, Alex, I swear I wasn't calling you."

"Oh, it was you, you just didn't realize it." I'm sure he could tell from my blank expression that I had no idea what he was talking about, so he pressed on.

"During the final call, you said the name, 'Sebastian'."

I started to correct him yet again, but he held up his hand to silence me.

"Six months ago, my friend and mentor, Sebastian Kess, went missing. He was assigned to apprehend an extremely dangerous criminal and had tracked him to Shenzhen, an industrial city in China. In his last communication, he requested additional personnel to aid in the arrest and was planning to hole up in a hotel until they arrived. He hasn't been heard from or seen since and everyone accepted the grim reality that he is likely dead. Your peculiar calls, coupled with the mention of his name, roused my suspicion. Using your cell number, I determined your name and address and came to Tucson to check it out."

My head was practically bursting with all the questions his revelation brought to mind. "Wait, so it's not a coincidence that you were in the bar? Have you been stalking me?"

He offered a sheepish half-grin. "Not exactly, but I have been keeping an eye on you the past few days. Who you hang out with, where you work, that kind of thing."

"I'm pretty sure that's the definition of stalking," I countered, starting to feel uncomfortable about this new piece of information.

"Perhaps it seems extreme, but I was concerned that you knew something about Sebastian. Or, at the very least, were trying to get help for him, but were prevented from openly asking for it. I couldn't judge the extent of your involvement, so I had to employ stealth to find out as much as possible. I certainly haven't been watching you for some nefarious purpose, which, I believe, is an integral component of being a stalker. In an case, it soon became apparent that you were an unlikely conspirator."

He seemed genuinely sincere, and if he had wanted to harm me, he certainly had ample opportunity in the last half hour or so.

"Okay," I said finally. "I don't think you're a stalker. But what did you mean when you said I didn't know that I was calling you? That doesn't make any sense. And how did you know that I had bought the Kindle?"

He looked at me with a thoughtful expression. "There's really no simple way to tell you what I need to tell you."

"Sure there is," I interrupted. "Just blurt it out."

"It's very complicated and will require you to change the entire way you view your world. I can't just blurt it out."

I couldn't imagine what he might tell me that would be so transformational. "Look, I'm hearing voices and I freaked out in front of a bar full of people. This has been one of the worst days of my life and I'm not in the mood for this. Stop being so damned dramatic, Alex, and just give me the abridged version."

"Sebastian is a powerful, magical being from another dimension whose essence was transferred to you through your Kindle."

The nice thing about losing your mind is that you can chalk up things like what Alex just said to insanity. I decided that, at least for the time being, I would accede to my wacked-out psyche and play along with the preposterous explanation.

"I changed my mind. I want the long version instead."

The corners of Alex's mouth lifted into a small smile. "The world you know is not the only one that exists. Sebastian and I come from another plane, if you will, where the people have what you would consider magical abilities."

"Uh-huh," I murmured, not bothering to mask my skepticism. "Can you make something disappear?"

As soon as the words left my lips, the chair upon which Alex was sitting disappeared, and he hadn't moved a muscle. Even more remarkable, perhaps, was that he was

41

still in exactly the same position as before the dematerialization occurred. I drew my hand through the space beneath his butt—fully expecting to feel the chair that surely was still there—but was shocked when it passed through unfettered.

"You aren't imagining it," Alex confirmed. "The chair's not there." With a wink, he added, "But, now it is." Sure enough, the rickety ladderback I bought for three bucks at a yard sale reappeared.

"How'd you do that?"

He shrugged. "Magic."

I should have been able to come up with something witty in response to the demonstration. Or, at the very least, some comment loaded with my usual snark. But all that came out was, "Damn."

Still not entirely convinced my mind wasn't playing tricks—albeit really, really elaborate ones—I asked Alex to perform another feat. He agreed, with one added parameter. He wrote out what he planned to do, and gave me the now folded note. Then, he glanced at Vinnie, fast asleep and oblivious to his master's apparent mental breakdown, and the cat began to slowly lift from the back of the loveseat where he had been draped in blissful slumber.

Vinnie woke with a start, clawing wildly at the air as he teleported across the room. His struggling stopped only when his paws touched the floor near the front door, he spat out one furious hiss, and dashed to the safety of the bedroom.

Trembling, I unfolded the paper. In neat cursive, the entire event had been described, right down to how high Vinnie would levitate and where he'd be deposited.

This had to be real. I wasn't nearly clever enough to craft *that* elaborate of a delusion.

"Okay," I conceded. "As screwy as all this seems, I believe you."

Alex offered a small, but obviously relieved, smile. "As I was saying, for millennia our worlds remained separated, except for a few isolated fissures that allowed passage from our dimension to yours. It required a huge output of magical energy to do so and even more to return. Only the most aged and powerful could accomplish such journeys. Thus, it was very uncommon. These gaps were used primarily as a means for banishing criminals; those convicted of heinous acts were given a choice between death and permanent exile."

"Sort of like Australia in the eighteenth century," I interjected.

"Except my ancestors thought that your dimension was devoid of any civilizations."

"It's not like the British considered the Aboriginal people to be civilized," I argued.

He let out an exasperated sigh. "Yes, but the practice was halted when it was discovered that beings similar to us, though non-magical, inhabited this dimension. It is considered a terrible, dark mark in our history and we are, to this day, deeply ashamed of our actions. Anyway, once your side industrialized, the ensuing pollution began to erode the barrier. For all intents and purposes, now there is no separation between the worlds. Any Coursodon can move freely back and forth, regardless of magical aptitude."

"Coursodon?"

"That is what we call ourselves. It's the equivalent of human."

He stood up and went to the kitchen. Opening a couple of cabinets, he rooted around before returning with a bottle of tequila in one hand and two small glasses in the other. By way of asking permission, he gestured with them and I gladly nodded in approval. Yep, this was definitely the sort of conversation that could only be improved with liquor.

Alex set the glasses on the table and poured a generous amount into each one. He handed one to me, which I drained before he had taken the other for himself. He chortled softly, and downed his in similar fashion.

Bolstered by the booze, I invited him to continue the tale.

"As you can imagine, beings with supernatural abilities can cause tremendous problems to those that lack these skills. The truth of our existence is known to only a few humans. Now that virtually any Courso can come and go as they please, we must ensure that travelers without the best intentions do not impose upon your dimension. We have specially trained *Xyzok*—enforcers that hunt and apprehend those who break your laws."

"So, Sebastian is one of these *Xyzok*?"

"Yes, one of the best."

"And it's his voice I heard?"

"Yes."

"And you know this because…?"

"When we passed on the running trail, I was almost certain I sensed Sebastian's magical signature. At that point, I assumed it was because you had recently been close to him. However, tonight in the bar, when you looked so stricken, I could actually *feel* Sebastian as I took your hands in mine. And then you called me by my Courso name; there is no way you would have randomly come up with that on your own."

I thought back to the moments before the voice and recalled saying something, but not knowing what it was. "That was your name? It didn't even sound like a word."

"Our real names are very difficult to pronounce. That's why we choose a human one to use while we are in this dimension."

I got up and poured myself another shot. Thankfully, the bottle was almost full, because there was no telling how much of the stuff I might need before the night ended. Steeling myself, I chugged the tequila, took a deep breath, and asked the million-dollar question.

"Okay, so how, exactly, did Sebastian get inside me?"

"When a human's life ends, their essence—or spirit, if you prefer—exists in another plane while the body dies. When Coursodon cease to be, their essence, their essential self, dies, but the body stays intact.

"That sounds like a waste of a lot of perfectly good bodies."

He nodded. "Sebastian thought exactly the same thing. Anyway, he has been studying what he called 'spiritual convergence' for many, many years. He believed that if one's essence was contained after it left the body, it could be preserved."

"Like formaldehyde for the soul?"

"That is one way to describe it," he replied, not bothering to hide his amusement.

"What do you do with all the bodies?" I asked.

The amused expression morphed into a confused one.

"If the bodies don't decompose, don't they start to pile up?" I offered in clarification.

"Ah," he said, nodding. "The bodies are buried, though technically, I suppose they don't have to be. Occasionally, someone with separation issues keeps the body of a loved one around because they can't seem to part with it." When he saw the revulsion on my face, he quickly added, "But that's very rare and is considered extremely bizarre behavior."

"So, the bodies are sort of like plastic soda containers; once the drink is consumed, the empties can last in a landfill forever."

Alex's forehead creased, and I was immediately sorry for the comparison. For all I knew, what I just said was considered blasphemy in Coursodon. I was surprised, however, when his face brightened and he said, "I suppose that's exactly what it is like."

I felt better not having insulted him. But, while all this metaphysical mumbo jumbo was interesting, I still needed to know what the hell was going on.

"Right," I drew out. "So back to Sebastian."

"When we came in physical contact at O'Reilly's, Sebastian managed to transmit bits of what happened. If you would allow me to do so again, I believe I can extract the entire explanation. Now that I have an idea of what is going on, I should be able to modulate the power surge so it won't be so unpleasant for you."

Oh sure, why the hell not? So far, my evening was already off the chart freaky, I might as well go all the way. I leaned forward and extended my hands toward his, then he placed his palms lightly over mine and closed his eyes. Where our hands met, I felt only a tingling sensation, rather than the concussion of energy from before. Alex's eyes twitched behind his lids, much like rapid eye movements when dreaming, but he wasn't asleep.

We remained like this for perhaps five minutes before he looked at me and grinned. I placed my hands in my lap and waited expectantly for the details.

"Sebastian was ambushed in his hotel room by Otto Kashanian, the thug he was sent to arrest. Gravely wounded, and without hope of being found before dying, he elected to test his theories of convergence as a last-ditch effort to stay alive. He encrypted his essence into binary code, intending to broadcast himself into his laptop, which was on and in the room. He predicted that his spiritual-self would remain intact and protected there until he could be reunited with his corporeal-self.

"Unfortunately, he believes that during the melee with Kashanian, the computer was damaged and no longer receiving data. There was a warehouse nearby, which he assumes to be a Kindle manufacturing site. Luckily for Sebastian, someone must have been testing the wireless capabilities of one just as he became disembodied, and he was intercepted by this," he said, picking up my Kindle.

He looked at the eBook reader with both wonder and admiration and whispered, "He did it. That crazy bastard actually did it."

I shouldn't have interrupted his obvious reverence, but couldn't contain myself. I vaguely recalled that data was transferred over the internet using the ones and zeros of binary code, but turning oneself into computer speak seemed unimaginable.

"How is that even possible?"

He stared at me for a long time. "Let me get this straight. You've accepted that you are essentially possessed by a supernatural being who trapped himself in your Kindle to avoid destruction by a sociopathic outlaw, but you are questioning if the process is *technically* feasible?"

"Well, it's a lot to wrap your head around all at once." I leaned back into the sofa, my elbows resting on each knee, and my now pounding head cradled in my hands. "I guess I'm more comfortable trying to understand what I can understand, understand?" I paused, suddenly overcome with consumer remorse. "Damn it, when the website said, *special offers*, I thought it just meant advertisements. Instead, I get a possessed eBook reader!"

He kneeled next to me, and gently placed a hand on my arm. "Are you sure you're alright? You're sort of babbling."

Truth be told, I was far from alright. Who would be prepared for this kind of shit? I could imagine the conversation at work on Monday:

"What did you do over the weekend, Hailey?"

"Not much, went to O'Reilly's, met a guy, was taken over by the man in my Kindle."

There were so many things I wanted to ask—I didn't know where to begin. Eventually, I settled on the one thing that seemed the most important.

"Can't he just put himself back in the Kindle?" I asked, my voice coming out small and shaky.

Alex frowned. "He doubts it, now that he has no physical body to help focus his power. It was difficult enough for him to compel you to dial my number and say a few words."

"Can you do it?"

"I don't know exactly how he accomplished this. We've discussed the concept, but without knowing the specifics, attempting to recreate the act could do great harm to both of you. It's too big a risk."

Alex seemed to sense that I was starting to panic at the thought of being permanently inhabited and added, "It's too risky *now*, but I promise you that I will find a way to disassociate the two of you."

"What am I supposed to do in the meantime?"

"You are going to get some rest." He helped me to my feet and guided me toward the bedroom. Pulling back the comforter, Alex sat me down on the bed, and took off my shoes.

"Tomorrow, I will try to channel some of my energy to Sebastian so that we can communicate more effectively. And then, we will formulate a plan." He cupped my chin in his large hand and I felt a pleasant wave of calm sweep through me.

"What was that?" I murmured sleepily as I stretched out on the bed.

He tucked the comforter around me, turned out the bedside lamp, and whispered, "Think of it as a paranormal Xanax."

~6~

After almost seven full hours of uninterrupted slumber, I awoke feeling rested and refreshed. If Alex could bottle whatever sleeping spell he used on me, he'd be rich.

I got up, brushed my teeth, washed my face, and went into the living room. The blanket that was usually draped over the end of my bed was stretched over the cushions of the sofa; Alex must have snagged it and slept on the couch. I glanced around—one could take in pretty much the whole place from where I was standing—and saw Alex, sitting on the back patio, petting Vinnie, who was curled up in his lap. Opening the sliding door, I took a deep breath of the crisp air, fragrant with the scents of the desert in winter.

Alex turned his head smiled. "Good morning. I trust you slept well?"

"Yeah, I did," I replied. "You know, I don't let Vinnie outside. Between the coyotes, bobcats, and birds of prey, there are too many things out there that could eat him."

"Sorry, I didn't even think about predators." Alex looked down at his furry companion with mock admonishment. "You were very insistent, but I won't let you dupe me again."

He ousted the cat from his lap and carried him into the house. It was unusual for Vinnie to cuddle up with a stranger, although, his behavior had been so strange lately, who knew what was going on in that little brain of his. Upon further consideration, however, another explanation occurred to me.

"Alex, does Sebastian like cats?"

"Hates them. Why?"

It was all starting to make sense. "Does he like rugby, red meat, and coffee with tons of cream and sugar?"

He looked at me suspiciously as he answered with a drawn out, "Yes ... why?"

"The last few days I have been doing all kinds of things I normally would never do and Vinnie has been acting like he's afraid I might kick him when he's not looking."

"Fascinating." Alex placed his thumb under his chin and tapped his forefinger against his nose, contemplated this new revelation. "That must be why you ordered Glen Fiddich last night. You really wanted tequila, didn't you? That's the only alcohol I found in your house."

"Yes, and every time I ate or drank something I normally wouldn't, I both loved and loathed it at the same time."

"Fascinating," he repeated. "You can experience his appetites, both victual and diversional."

"You know, Alex," I observed, "You have a very old-fashioned way of expressing yourself sometimes."

"Really? I try to keep up with the evolution of your language, but sometimes it is easy to overlook the finer points. What did I say that was anachronistic?"

"Well, anachronistic, for one. And, no one uses the word 'victual'." Then, I recalled our original phone conversation. "You called me 'toots', too. I think my great-grandfather used to call me that. Did you learn English from a book written in the nineteen-thirties?" I said teasingly.

"No, I learned English in the nineteen-thirties."

I don't know why that tidbit should have thrown me off. After all, I had come to grips with the idea another world coexisted with ours. It really shouldn't have bothered me that instead of Alex being somewhere around my age, he was way older. Probably way, way so.

"Exactly how old are you?" I asked.

He turned around and headed to the kitchen. "One hundred and twenty-four," he called out over his shoulder. "You hungry? I could make pancakes."

"Whoa!" I exclaimed. "You can't just say 'a hundred and twenty-four' and then blithely discuss breakfast." I stared at him, my mouth hanging open, trying to comprehend that he had already experienced three different centuries but he looked thirty—tops.

"I know it's shocking; I bet you're thinking I don't look a day over one hundred."

When I didn't laugh, he offered a more serious explanation. "We age at a much slower rate than humans. Physiologically, I'm the equivalent of a twenty-five or thirty-year-old." He grinned mischievously and added, "Think of it as dog years in reverse."

I shook my head slowly. *What's that make their normal lifespan, like, three or four hundred?*

"Okay, Fido," I said finally. "Let's make some victuals."

Surprisingly, I had all the ingredients necessary for Alex to prepare pancakes. The only item I was missing was the maple syrup, but I did have some apricot jam my mother sent at Christmas. She claimed the brand— Heavenly Preserved—was especially delicious because all the fruit was grown organically and prayed over while ripening on the trees. Despite my skepticism that religious fervor could influence produce, as well as the company's motto—*Delicious because you can taste the Jesus in it!*—it was quite tasty.

After stuffing ourselves and cleaning up, it was time to attempt a more efficient method for brainstorming with Sebastian. Alex explained that, while he could communicate with Sebastian through our physical contact, it would be more productive if whatever Sebastian wanted to say could come directly out of me. I was initially reluctant to be his mouthpiece, but eventually saw the sense in having a less roundabout way for them to confer.

As we had the night before, Alex and I assumed our positions across from one another. This time, I opted to rest my upturned palms on my knees instead of outstretched in front of me, as my arms still ached from last night's session. We touched, and after a while, the electrical buzziness morphed into more of a relaxing hum. I even started to nod off once or twice.

Alex finally pulled his hands away, leaned back in the chair and closed his eyes for a few moments. When he finally spoke, he said wearily, "That was much more draining than I imagined."

"Fortunately, I feel quite rejuvenated."

I jumped at the sound of the voice. "Shit," I shrieked. "Did that come out of my mouth, or is he still just in my head?"

"Well, the profanity was loud and clear, but other than that, I didn't hear anything" Alex said, frowning. "Evidently, my efforts were unsuccessful."

"Tell Alexander that while he failed to achieve direct verbal communication using your vocal chords, he did manage to significantly enhance my ability to communicate with you."

I relayed the info. "Apparently, you only made it easier for him to talk in my head."

Alex tried twice more to accomplish his original goal, both sessions ended without a favorable outcome. Ultimately, Alex accepted the limitation me as a conduit. The good news was now Sebastian didn't have to work very hard to communicate with me. The bad news was he felt the need to verbalize whatever popped into his mind. Now, instead of an occasional, unexpected word or two, I was bombarded with a running commentary about anything and everything. He had an opinion about the color of my throw pillows, for fuck's sake.

It wasn't long before I'd had enough, and insisted he limit himself to speaking only when he had something important to say. Maybe he was just making up for the months of forced silence, because he did tone it down once I complained.

By the time the afternoon became evening, Alex and Sebastian had formulated a plan. Sebastian believed that it would be easiest for his essence to return to his own body, as it was already configured for him. They hoped that using their considerable web of contacts, they could determine if it could be located, and if so, if its condition was such that reconvergence was possible.

The alternative approach was inserting Sebastian into a different physical form. This scenario was problematic for a number of reasons, not the least of which was the necessity for a suitable dead guy being available when he and I separated. As neither Alex nor Sebastian intended to kill someone for their body, they agreed that finding Sebastian's was the best strategy.

My stomach started to grumble, and I realized we'd skipped lunch entirely. Alex wanted to stop by his hotel to get his laptop, so we decided to go out for dinner beforehand. We went to one of my favorite places, a small hole-in-the-wall diner that looked so seedy from the outside no one who valued their health would venture in without a prior recommendation.

As usual, Pancho's was crowded, but we lucked out when a table for two became available after a short wait. The joint was open twenty-four/seven/three sixty-five. In fact, they didn't even have locks on the doors because they never closed. The menu items spanned everything from eggs to enchiladas and the clientele included college professors, motorcycle gangs, and suburban housewives. Even the mayor ate there.

I knew the menu by heart, but grabbed one for Alex before we sat down.

"What do you recommend?" Alex asked after a few minutes of study.

"Hopefully, something without Salmonella," Sebastian groused. *"I have no desire to watch you retch out dinner later tonight."*

"Lighten up. I've eaten here for years, and I've never had a problem."

Alex looked up from his menu. "Let me guess, Sebastian objects to the less than five-star ambiance."

"He's worried about food poisoning. You know, Sebastian, you really are a snob."

"It is not snobbery to be concerned about the sanitary conditions of one's surroundings. But do not mind me; it is your gastrointestinal tract."

The waitress came by, glanced appreciatively at Alex, and asked if I was having my usual— huevos rancheros and an iced tea. I smiled and nodded, and Alex ordered the same for himself. Sebastian remained mostly silent, only complaining when I refused to add sugar to my tea.

The food came quickly, and we enthusiastically dug into the warm, spicy layers of refried beans, eggs, cheese, and salsa that topped crisp, corn tortillas.

"This is fantastic," Alex murmured, spooning more salsa onto his plate. "What do you think, Sebastian? Ambrosial, yes?"

Sebastian must have been sulking because his only comment was a huffing sound. Just as well. I was too busy stuffing my face to deal with his issues.

After sharing a chocolate tamal for dessert, we made our way to the hotel. Alex was booked into one of those industrial-strength places—clean with few frills. His room, which was on the third floor, had a passable view of the Santa Catalina Mountains that spanned the north end of town. Four mountain ranges surrounded Tucson: the Catalinas, the Rincons, the Santa Ritas, and the Tucson Mountains. All had somewhat different topography and elevations, but all were beautiful.

Glancing around the impersonal surroundings, I said, "It seems silly for you to pay for a hotel room. If you don't mind the couch, you can stay at my place. Besides, it'll be easier for you and Sebastian to strategize if you don't waste time going back and forth."

I'm not sure why I extended the invite, but I didn't feel like Sebastian had a role in it. It wasn't like I made a habit of asking guys I barely knew to move in, but then again, I didn't make a habit of sharing my body with the spiritual essence of a guy from a parallel dimension, either. The whole bizarre mess did seem not so messy when Alex was around, however.

"Thanks, Hailey. If you are sure I won't be intruding, that would probably simplify things."

He began to put clothes and such into a small duffle that had been on the end of one of the twin beds. When he finished, he slung the bag over one shoulder and grabbed the laptop before we went downstairs so he could check out.

Back at the guesthouse, I cleared off a section of the counter in the bathroom and gathered a towel and some bedding for him. I didn't really have anything to use as a dresser in the living room, but I moved some paperbacks onto the floor so he could use the now empty shelves for his stuff.

Remembering I'd skipped showering that morning, I excused myself, got some clean clothes from my bedroom, and went into the bathroom. I turned on the water to let it heat up, and as I started to take off my clothes, I happened to glance at myself in the mirror.

Son of a bitch! If Sebastian could tell that Pancho's looked like a dump, he could see what I could. There was no way in hell I'd be comfortable taking a shower knowing that he'd get an eyeful of me, naked.

Frantically wracking my brain for a solution, I settled on the only thing that seemed to make sense. I turned out the lights. The little glow from the clock radio on the shelf above the toilet emitted too much illumination, so I threw a washcloth over it. That was better; I could barely see anything, and figured I was safe. I removed my clothes, pulled back the shower curtain, and adjusted the water temperature before climbing in.

When finished, I shut off the water and stood there dripping. *Shit.* In my haste to eliminate any chance of supernatural voyeurism, I had forgotten to put the bath towel on the hook next to the shower. I pushed open the curtain, carefully lifting one leg over the side of the tub. Damn, it was dark. Pivoting to make my way to the other side of the bathroom where the towel was located, I slipped. Without any visual landmarks to guide me, I reflexively grabbed the closest thing to me to prevent myself from falling, which happened to be the shower curtain. The vinyl drape tore from the hooks, plunging both it and me to the floor.

"Are you alright in there?" Alex shouted from the other side of the bathroom door.

If I'd been smart, I would have answered him immediately. Instead, I tried to disentangle myself from the wet, plastic mess that now surrounded me.

Alex burst through the door, the light from the hallway illuminating the jumble of my naked self, sprawled on the tile, atop the now shredded shower curtain.

I had to give him high marks; he turned around almost immediately. Chivalrous, perhaps, but his shoulders shook as he tried, with only moderate success, to stifle the laughter that threatened to overwhelm him.

"You seem to fall down a lot," he finally managed to say.

"Just toss me the towel, please," I croaked out in embarrassment.

He complied, and I wrapped myself in the terrycloth before pulling myself off the floor. Now that I was upright, it was apparent no serious damage occurred—a few places were going to be bruised, but my body escaped relatively intact. I couldn't say the same for my ego, however.

"Did the bulb burn out?" Alex asked as I swept past him and into my bedroom.

Slamming the door behind me, I quickly threw on some clothes. I planned to salvage as much dignity as possible by acting as if showering in the dark and falling in a heap on the floor was an everyday occurrence, but knew I couldn't pull it off. Reluctantly, I emerged from my fortress of humiliation, hoping by some miracle Alex had developed amnesia and had forgotten the last few minutes. Or, at the very least, had decided to take a long walk to allow me time to wallow privately in my mortification. No such luck, because there he was, leaning against the bathroom doorframe, arms crossed over his chest, and a huge grin on his face.

"Oh crap," I moaned, using my hands to hide the bright red flush I knew had crawled up my cheeks. I peeked out between my fingers and looked up into his vivid blue eyes, which now conveyed more concern than mirth. "I didn't want Sebastian to see me naked," I confessed, "so, I turned out the lights."

Alex considered my explanation. "I'm fairly certain that if Sebastian had wanted to observe you unclothed he had ample opportunity. Besides, if he only sees what you can, you could have simply closed your eyes."

"He has a point, my dear. And while I may be many things, a degenerate I am not. I shall respect your privacy, as much as possible, given the extraordinary circumstances in which we find ourselves ensnared."

"Thanks, Sebastian. I appreciate that. So, besides being able to see through my eyes and talk in my head, what else can you make me do?"

"I can also sense your physiologic changes, like when you are hungry, or upset, but I cannot force you to do anything."

"You made me phone Alex and say his real name," I protested.

"Yes, but even those minor acts required a tremendous amount of magical energy. In my present form—or lack thereof, to be more precise—I am only capable of limited compelling spells. Although under normal circumstances, I could make you do all sorts of things without your consent, if I so desired."

While I could only hear Sebastian, I got the distinct impression there was a wink at the end of that last comment. I ignored the innuendo.

"Okay, what about the scotch and the sugar-loaded coffee?"

"I believe that in those instances, your body was reacting to my preferences. I craved Glen Fiddich, and that trickled over to you."

"You believe?" I snapped. "I'd feel a lot better about this if you had more to go on than just conjecture."

Sebastian snapped back. *"Don't take that tone with me. This is the first time I have accomplished this. It's all conjecture at this point."*

My indignation was growing exponentially. "I bet you make me trip the first time I saw Alex."

"I wanted to be certain that you established contact. I couldn't let you just jog past each other."

I started to give my arrogant body-mate a particularly curse-filled piece of my mind, but Alex interrupted. He hadn't heard Sebastian's side of the argument, but got the gist from my end.

"You know, Hailey, Sebastian feels terrible about what has happened and obviously never meant for you to be caught up in all this. Your safety, skinned knees notwithstanding, is his utmost concern. He may be pretentious and self-absorbed, but he is also extremely ethical and conscientious."

Now I felt humiliated *and* presumptuous. I prided myself on objectivity, and here I was, making assumptions.

I realized that I knew very little about Sebastian, which seemed unfortunate given that we were cohabitating. Literally.

"You're right, Alex. Sebastian, I'm sorry I was so bitchy."

No one said anything for a while, and the silence only made the uncomfortable situation more so. Using the age-old strategy of changing the subject to dispel the awkwardness, I said, "Alex, tell me about Sebastian. You mentioned that he was your mentor?"

"Yes, I was lucky enough to be his apprentice for many years before we became partners. He taught me everything I know."

"I suppose that means he's older than you?"

"Quite a bit. I'm not certain of his exact age, but he's at least two hundred and forty years old."

At first, I envisioned some old, wrinkly codger. Then, I realized if Alex looked the way he did at a hundred and twenty-four, Sebastian probably appeared no more than middle-aged. I made a mental note to make sure I grilled them both about various historical events. What a boon to be able to get information from someone who was alive during the constitutional convention or the Civil War.

"What sorts of things did he teach you?" I asked, trying to stay on topic.

Alex settled on the sofa before he answered. "All Courso are born with some type of magical aptitude, but most excel at only one or two specialties. Some are gifted healers, some have a talent for more physical manifestations. Whatever their natural proclivities, they need to be nurtured and developed. It's the same with humans; if you have a skill, you get training to improve your abilities. Sebastian and I are unusual in that we are both proficient in a multitude of areas—Sebastian extraordinarily so. As a boy, I was sent to live with him so that he could help me reach my full potential."

"Sort of like boarding school for the magically

gifted," I remarked.

He smiled ruefully. "Yes, but I was the only student."

"That must have been lonely. Didn't you miss your parents?"

"I got to spend holidays with them," he said with a shrug. "And having Sebastian as a teacher was amazing. He rarely accepts apprentices. When I became an adult, he continued to train me as a *Xyzok*."

"You hunt Courso bad guys, too?"

"Yes. The *Xyzok* are a specialized force that hunt Coursodon that prey upon humans. We have two main duties: to apprehend or eliminate those of our kind that use magic to harm humans and to keep our existence hidden from the public. There's a separate agency that's responsible for internal law enforcement; you know, crimes of Courso on Courso."

Keep their existence hidden? "Am I in some sort of danger because I know about Coursodon?"

"Oh no, of course not. There's no problem with small numbers of people becoming aware of us. But we are hesitant to make our presence known on a wide scale until we are certain that humans can accept us. No point in drumming up trouble."

I had to admit that I couldn't fault that logic. Throughout history, humans had enough difficulty accepting the relatively minor differences between cultures and races. It was hard to imagine the chaos that might ensue if we had to deal with supernaturals.

"Maybe in the next century," I remarked sarcastically. "And frankly, I wouldn't wager any money on it happening that soon."

"Yes, humans can be quite resistant to change," he agreed. "They cling so tenaciously to their beliefs, even when faced with ample evidence that they are incorrect. On the other hand, one of the things that I find so appealing about humans is that same resolve when it comes to ideals that should never be altered. It is, in a sense, one of humanity's best, and at the same time, worst qualities."

While I pondered the philosophical ramifications of Alex's comments, Sebastian decided to reinsert himself into the conversation.

"Alexander has always been so cerebral about such things. Change occurs whether one accepts it or not. The only difference is how much energy one expends during the journey."

"He says you're over thinking the whole stubborn human thing."

Alex chortled softly. "Sebastian is uncomfortable with the complexities of life."

"He is mistaken, my dearest Hailey. I revel in complexity. It is the complicated that I abhor. Complex implies order with intricacy. Complicated involves convolution. Those are the subtleties that Alexander does not embrace."

I was beginning to get tired of repeating what Sebastian was saying back to Alex. "Hey, don't get me in the middle of some metaphysical pissing contest," I protested. "It's bad enough having someone else's voice in my head, I can't be expected to always be Sebastian's official spokesperson, too. You guys want to debate the fine distinctions between words and concepts, do it when you are hooked up and leave me out of it."

"Of course, do forgive me. But please, try not to get those lovely, pink lace panties of yours in a wad over it."

"My pink lace what?" I sputtered.

"I am sorry, is that not the proper terminology—panties in a wad? Modern slang can be so cumbersome."

I *had* put on a fuchsia thong after the shower incident. "How did you … wait, you said you were too gallant to look."

"I said I am not a degenerate. I do not, however, lack normal masculine proclivities. I admit—I peeked. However, you should not be self-conscious, my dear, you are quite lovely. And that is truly a great compliment, considering I have been with thousands of women."

Alex scowled in response to the one-sided

conversation, but I was pretty sure he got the salient points, because he uttered an accusatory, "Sebastian…?" in a clipped tone.

"Oh whatever," I tossed out in resignation. Great, now everyone had seen me naked today. "I'm tired. I'm going to bed."

I looked expectantly at Vinnie, who had been lounging atop of one of the bookshelves, hoping he might follow me into my room. Instead, he gave me one of those typically feline looks that expressed something akin to "hell no," jumped onto the couch and began rubbing his head enthusiastically against Alex's arm.

Alex shrugged. "I'm sure he's just a bit put off by Sebastian's aura."

"Yeah," I said, as I headed off for the bedroom. "Me and him both."

The rest of the weekend passed without too many problems. Alex continued to email various associates in and around Shenzhen, where Sebastian had been attacked, to determine if his body could be located. If we found it, Alex and I would travel there and try to complete the reconvergence.

Alex and Sebastian spent a good part of Sunday planning how to proceed, leaving me relegated to duty as their communication channel. It was weird sitting there, palm to palm with Alex for hours at a time without speaking, but eventually it became clear that as long I wasn't talking, I could engage in other activities without disturbing the connection.

I still couldn't bring myself to use the Kindle, although I wasn't sure why. What were the chances of something other than literature popping out now that Sebastian had been unleashed? I did get a chance to watch one of my all-time favorite movies, *The Princess Bride*, as well as some English Premier League soccer, which both Alex and Sebastian enjoyed.

On Monday, I went to work with Alex in tow. He said it was a good idea if he thought of something he needed to talk about with Sebastian, but secretly, I think he was just worried that leaving us unchaperoned could result in World War III.

We had to fabricate a cover story to explain who Alex was and why he was coming to work. Most of what we came up with ranged from incredibly lame—Alex was an old friend from out of town, who had always wanted to see what I did for a living—to merely lame—I met him at the bar and invited him to come to work with me because he thought I was bullshitting him about milking chinchilla. That part was entirely believable—Alex *had* been incredulous when I admitted I didn't work at a normal dairy, as did most people when they learned the truth about my absurd career—and we finally settled on a version of the latter scenario: I met Alex at O'Reilly's and it turned out he was a computer whiz who I hired to help revamp our outdated computer systems. My co-workers might question how we met, as I wasn't one to strike up conversations with strangers, but they would be pleased I'd finally decided to upgrade the technology in the office. And the fact that Alex was hot wouldn't bother Rachel and Chelsea too much, either.

As was my custom, we arrived before everyone else, and Alex made coffee while I opened the barriers for the critters. While the coffee brewing, he peered out the window from the office to the playroom, watching what I was doing with rapt bemusement.

"Honestly, even when we got here, I was still convinced that you were making all this up," he admitted when I returned to the office. "There's actually money to be made in chinchilla milk cheese?"

I slid past him and plunked down in my chair before answering.

"The company makes all kinds of more traditional cheeses at other locations that keep the business in the black. They don't make a profit on the chinchilla milk products, but it attracts people to the other stuff," I explained. "The chinchilla cheese is really, really expensive because they don't give much milk. People usually only buy it on a lark."

"I'm sure no party is complete without the chinchilla milk cheese spread," he teased. "How did you become a chinchilla milk maid, anyway?"

"The lab that I used to work in did nutritional research, and we used rat milk for some of the experiments. You can't just buy that sort of thing online, and I became the rat milker. It wasn't a skill I figured would ever help on my resume, but someone from the university heard the business wanted to expand its line to the more exotic, and recommended me. The rest, as they say, is history."

He seemed to be letting all that sink in, staring at me as he tapped his fingers on the desk. Finally, he asked, "Is this something that you enjoy?"

"Well, I like the critters and the people at work." Not really a rousing endorsement, but in truth, I didn't see myself making a lifetime career of it. "I suppose someday I'll figure out what I want to do when I grow up," I joked.

I heard the front door open and in came Chelsea and Daniel, with Rachel following close behind. Rachel was regaling them with specifics of Harrison's weekend bout with food poisoning that would make a physician hurl. I thought Daniel and Chelsea were trying to stay ahead of her to avoid hearing more of the disgusting details, but Rachel was oblivious to their obvious discomfort. As fantastic as Rachel was, she did tend to over-share.

Fortunately for us all, as soon as she saw a stranger, she didn't finish her newest comment, which had started with, "And the grossest part was when …"

I introduced Alex and explained that he was here to make the computers and software more efficient. As he began to boot up one of the desktops on the other side of the room, Rachel slid next to me and whispered, "Niiiiice. Where'd you find the hot geek?"

Confronted with my friend's salacious tone, the meeting-in-the-bar story, while true, now seemed like a bad choice. I was trying to come up with a reasonable alternative when Alex, whose back was to us while he scrutinized the computer screen, piped in with, "We met at O'Reilly's on Friday night."

Rachel raised an eyebrow but said nothing. I knew that as soon as we were alone, however, she would pepper me with more questions.

As she walked over to the coffee pot to pour herself a mug-full, Sebastian let out a long, drawn out, "*Mmmm*," before adding, "*My, my. That is a magnificent woman. Simply exquisite.*"

I wanted to tell him to shut up, but stopped myself before I had to explain why I blurted out a complete non-sequitur. Instead, I continued to smile at Rachel while Sebastian persisted in extolling her beauty. When his prattle became unbearable, I retreated to the relative privacy of the large, walk-in storage refrigerator before I let him have it.

"Shut. The. Fuck. Up," I seethed. "I don't want to hear how fantastic Rachel would look naked!"

"*Tsk, Tsk, my dear, such language. I apologize for offending your delicate sensibilities.*"

"I thought we discussed this before we left the house. You can't just babble on in my head while I'm around other people, and particularly not about Rachel. Try to restrain yourself."

"*In the future, I shall keep my thoughts on matters involving your friend private,*" he said, somewhat apologetically.

"Not just that—try to keep quiet unless there is something important you need to say." Given that Sebastian was so freaking old, it was surprising *I* took on the parental role in our relationship.

Returning to the office, I found Alex and Daniel animatedly discussing firewalls. As I had little interest in the topic, I left them to their conversation and went about my morning duties. By lunchtime, I managed to avoid the inevitable interrogation from Rachel, and Sebastian had been silent since our confrontation in the cooler. *Oh, happy days!*

We had sandwiches delivered from a nearby café and Chelsea and Rachel grilled Alex while we ate. Oh sure, they tried to make it seem like friendly chitchat, but I knew better. They were trying to do some exploratory reconnaissance to determine his dating potential, for my benefit, I presumed.

Alex seemed unfazed by the whole thing and earnestly answered their questions. Well, as much as he could, considering we were both skirting the truth. It wasn't as if either of us could tell them what was really going on. The thought of explaining that I harbored the essence of Alex's magically gifted, ex-mentor who was previously trapped in my newly purchased Kindle, was still tough for me to completely except.

Shortly before it was time to finish up for the day, Rachel finally cornered me.

"Alex is a really nice guy," she began while we checked the day's production. When I simply nodded in agreement, she continued with, "So, what happened at O'Reilly's? You expect me to believe that you just happened to strike up a conversation with a gorgeous guy with computer skills, who was currently between jobs? Spill it. I want details, girl."

"I know, but it was just a lucky coincidence," I said, nervously adjusting my hair sticks. I tried to sound as sincere as possible, but I hated lying to her. I did, however, opt for some honesty with my next comment. "He is pretty great, though."

"Uh, yeah he is," she joked, using her best imitation of a blonde airhead. "I hope you are giving him a chance; I think he likes you. I saw him watching you a lot today when he thought no one would notice."

I knew that the surveillance was likely a consequence of the situation with Sebastian, but I had to admit the thought of Alex being interested in me was appealing. *Wow. Me, Hailey Parrish, after swearing off the opposite sex for so long, was actually interested in a man.* Well, not a man exactly, but close enough.

Not wanting to give Rachel too much encouragement, I didn't admit my attraction outright, but replied, "I will definitely consider giving him a chance."

Rachel stuck her tongue out at me before walking away.

Intelligent, handsome, sensitive, and funny, Alex was close to the perfect guy—if you overlooked the whole, being from another dimension angle. And, truly, the non-human bit was kind of a turn-on—who knew what supernatural, erotic tricks he might have up his sleeve, or down his pants for that matter. I continued with this line of thought until Sebastian interrupted my fantasies.

"Rachel is very perceptive. I know Alexander well, and his attraction to you is unmistakable."

As soon as he related this observation, I could feel my face start to flush. It was like being back in middle school. *Oooh, does Johnny like me?* I was not only blushing, but immensely disgusted with myself for doing so, and relieved Sebastian couldn't read my mind, given what I had been thinking about moments before. Still, I had to stifle the smile that threatened to bust out from simply considering the prospects with Alex.

After work, Alex and I stopped at the grocery store and stocked up on food, all of which Alex paid for. I tried to protest, but he was adamant about doing his share. Once back at my place, we unloaded everything and started on dinner.

We had planned to use the grill, but it started to drizzle and neither of us wanted to stand in the rain while barbequing the chicken. Eventually, I decided to make pasta instead. I prepared the fresh tomato and basil sauce while Alex monitored the linguini for al dente-ness as it cooked. We added salad and some garlic bread, and ended up with a tasty meal.

During dinner, Alex explained that while not all his contacts had reported back, the ones that did hadn't discovered anything useful. No body was found in the hotel room, nor anywhere in the city in the days following the attack. This made him speculate that Kashanian or his minions had moved Sebastian.

"What if they buried or burned him? I asked as I chewed on my second garlicy roll.

"Either way, someone should still be able to detect his spectral trail," Alex replied. I had no idea what that meant and Alex must have sensed my confusion, because after a short pause, he continued with a more thorough explanation. "All of us have a unique magical signature, much like a DNA profile, that can be used for identification."

"Or under the circumstances, more like a supernatural IP address."

Alex laughed heartily at my sarcasm. "That's just the kind of caustic remark that Sebastian would make. But I doubt they would have tried to burn him—burying or concealing the body would attract less attention."

He remained hopeful that Sebastian's corporeal-self would be found in a state conducive to accepting the part of his mentor that was now in me. Me too—I didn't want to think about the alternatives.

Living alone for so long, I thought I was content with the solitude, but now that I had a roommate—or two, counting Sebastian—I realized that I missed the companionship. It was kind of nice having someone else around. We spent the rest of the evening talking and laughing about mostly inconsequential things: modern music, social networking, the inexplicable upsurge of hookah bars. If it had been a date, it would have been a good one.

We parted around eleven o'clock—I to my bedroom, Alex to the bathroom to shower. As I lay in bed, I heard him shut off the water and move about for a while. Eventually, the living room light clicked off and the house fell silent. I went to sleep listening to the soft, pitter-patter of rain on the roof, wondering what it might be like to have Alex here with me, instead of out on the couch with Vinnie.

~8~

I awoke feeling amazingly turned on. One hand was moving up and down between my legs, while the other was yanking my camisole top up to gain better access to my now erect nipples. I knew immediately this was not a manifestation of my own urges—I sometimes had sexy dreams, but they never made me feel myself up in my sleep.

"Damn it, Sebastian," I snarled, springing to a sitting position. "Stop making me do whatever it is you are doing right now."

"I swear, I am not making you do it, it is your physical reaction to my... needs."

"Your needs?" I hissed as I straightened my clothes.

"I cannot help it; I am a very sexual person. Normally, I have carnal relations at least once a day. And it has been months."

I leaned back onto the pillows and let out a long breath. "This is absurd."

"Why, pray tell, is this problematic? It is no different than if you had an erotic dream. This way, we both get the benefits."

"Except I don't have to deal with my fantasies once I wake up. I won't be able to look you, uh, myself in the eye afterwards. It's too ... icky."

"You could have sex with someone else. That would satisfy my cravings."

"I am not going to sleep with some guy just so you can get your rocks off."

"While I am not theoretically opposed to sexual liaisons with members of the same sex, I was thinking more along the lines of you sleeping with a woman. That friend of yours, Rachel, would be perfect. Her breasts are sublime."

"Are you insane?" I wanted to scream, but tried to keep my voice down to not disturb Alex. "I will not be your psychic fuck buddy. First, I'm straight. Second, do you think I would dupe a friend of mine into some sort of weird, supernatural threesome because you can't keep your pants zipped?

"Well, really they are your pants."

I rolled my eyes and took a deep, calming breath. "Look Sebastian, I understand how frustrating this must be for you, but you are a guest in my body, and I would appreciate it if you could take a mental cold shower when you are aroused."

There was a long silence and I wondered if he was sulking. Eventually he said, *"Fine. But if you hear me counting backwards by sevens, at least do me the courtesy of appreciating my sacrifice."*

I heard a soft rap at my door, and Alex called out, "Is everything okay in there?"

So much for keeping quiet. As long as he was up, I was tempted to tell him about Sebastian's sleazy proposal, but decided to take the high road instead.

"I'm fine. Just setting down a few ground rules. Sorry to have woken you."

He seemed like he might inquire more about what ground rules needed setting because he paused before he finally said, "No problem. Goodnight, Hailey."

***

I made it through the rest of the night without any interruptions. In fact, I heard little from Sebastian throughout the rest of week except for an occasional plaintive sigh when in the presence of Rachel. Which really was just fine with me; if Sebasatyr wanted to pout, he could go right ahead.

Alex came to work every day, and the only problem we encountered was when, on Tuesday morning, Rachel pulled me aside and asked why he and I had arrived in my car. Thinking we'd dotted all the i's and crossed all the t's, ruse-wise, the silly mistake could have been a problem. Fortunately, I came up with a plausible explanation—Alex's car was in the shop and he asked me if I could pick him up—and Rachel seemed satisfied with the story. It probably helped that I updated Alex when she wasn't around, so when Rachel interrogated him later, our stories matched. From then on, he drove his rental instead of carpooling with me. It was a huge waste of energy, to be sure, but it beat having my friends think I was shacking-up with a guy I had met only a few days before.

By Friday afternoon, Alex had improved our record keeping so that all the information from the microchips implanted in our herd could be accessed in a slick spreadsheet on our computers. As he explained it, investigators do most of their groundwork over the internet these days and he taught himself the art of data management when he realized that he spent too much time looking for information he'd already compiled. Thanks to Alex, our weekly paperwork decreased by about 50% and he did it for free. If nothing else, when this whole disembodied essence debacle was over, maybe I'd get a nice raise for my mad managerial skills.

Not only was Alex a fine pseudo-employee, he was also a great houseguest. He helped with the cooking and the cleaning, and paid for the groceries. Much to his credit—and my relief—he never mentioned the shower incident, even though he ran out to Wal-Mart to get a new curtain. Best of all, he never left the toilet seat up.

Rachel invited me, Chelsea, Daniel, and Alex to join her and Harrison at a new vegetarian restaurant that had recently opened downtown, named Café Sin Vacas. While none of us shunned meat, we were always up for trying something new, and Rachel heard the food was excellent.

We agreed to meet there later, and Alex and I drove off separately to maintain our deception. We took slightly different routes back to my place, a maneuver suggested by Alex, who insisted that if we were going to go to the trouble to take our own cars, we should make certain our subterfuge was thorough. Alex arrived before I did, and by the time I made it into the house, he was already in the bathroom.

While I waited for my turn, the song, *She Drives Me Crazy* by Fine Young Cannibals rang out from my cell phone. I had programmed that ring tone to identify only one caller and thought long and hard about ignoring it. Finally, I sucked it up and answered with as cheerful a tone as I could muster.

"Hi Mom."

"Hailey? Is that you?"

I rolled my eyes. Instead of asking her who else she thought would be answering my phone, I curbed the sarcasm and confirmed my identity.

"Oh, hello dear. I hadn't spoken to you in a while and I just wanted to check in to make sure you're alright."

It had been about two weeks since our last conversation, but contrary to my mother's assessment, that seemed like not nearly enough time between calls to me. "I'm good. What's new with you?"

"You would not believe what I've been through this week," she said. "I've had plumbers here three times, and they still haven't been able to fix the water pressure problem. Of course, they want to charge me whether they make the repairs or not. I'm sure they're Godless heathens; a true believer would never try to swindle someone."

"I thought you only employ repairmen you find on www.whowouldjesushire.net," I muttered idly.

"I do, but if I was a faithless huckster who wanted to cheat the righteous, that's just where I would place an advertisement."

There she goes; thirty seconds in, and she's already spouting anti-Christian conspiracy theories.

"Mom, I seriously doubt they are colluding against you. They are probably just bad plumbers." It was never a good idea to engage in this kind of repartee with my mother, and I decided to change the subject. "How's Dad?"

"Oh, same as usual. He squanders most of the day tinkering with his projects in the garage."

For years, my father coped with my mother's ever-increasing zealotry by spending a good portion of his free time as far away from her as possible. Lately, he had converted a portion of the garage into a workshop. He made various woodcrafts that he sold at farmer's markets around Branson, Missouri, where he and my mom had retired about five years before. I was convinced that the only thing that kept my parent's marriage intact was the fact that they rarely spent any time together.

My mother continued to drone on about my father's lack of religious conviction and I retreated to my usual state of tuning her out. I was quite adept at giving the appearance of paying attention, interjecting a well-timed "uh-huh" or "really?" with practiced aplomb.

As I continued to pay the bare minimum of attention, Alex emerged from the bathroom. A bath sheet was wrapped low around his hips, and the moisture that clung to his bare skin accentuated his well-developed chest and abs. His face, obscured by the second towel he used to dry his hair, allowed my undetected ogling of his sinewy muscles in response to the vigorous motion, as well as some fairly prominent scars that zigzagged across his torso and arms. I was so entranced, I didn't notice when he finished and caught me staring. To make matters worse, the distraction had also broken my concentrated non-concentration on my mother's blather.

"Are you listening to me, Hailey?" My mother's annoyance practically oozed out of the phone.

"Uh, sorry. I'm just a little preoccupied this evening." *Yeah, by a mostly naked hunk that is currently grinning like a Cheshire Cat.* I turned my back to him and said, "Continue, please," into the phone.

"Really, you'd think a daughter would be more interested in what is going on in her mother's life. I won't be around forever, you know. You should be thankful that you have a mother to talk to." She paused briefly and I could swear I heard a small, maudlin sob before she continued. "You're my only child," she said tremulously. "Would it hurt to pay attention occasionally?"

I closed my eyes and took a deep breath. "Mom, you have four other kids."

"Yes, but your sisters hate me. I consider you the only one."

My head was beginning to ache and I used my thumbs to put pressure on my temples to quell the mounting discomfort.

"Okay, Mom. This is ridiculous. Sarah, Teresa, Nina, and Allysa don't hate you. *No, they're just fed up with all your crap.* "I really have to get going. I'm meeting some friends for dinner."

Remarkably recovered from her melancholy of just moments before, she launched into her usual diatribe concerning my lack of a husband and the inevitable winding down of my biological clock. Actually, all I heard was, "You know, you only have a few fertile years left …" when I lied and said that Rachel was in the driveway and had to go. I disconnected and let out a long, frustrated shriek.

"I take it you and your mother don't get along?" Alex inquired.

I unclenched my fists, hoping that would help release the tension that was often the byproduct of interaction with the woman who gave birth to me. "Saying we don't get along is an understatement," I answered. "My mother is a difficult woman. We really have nothing in common except DNA."

I stomped into the bathroom, and spent the next few minutes trying to calm down. When I felt I was no longer likely to break anything, I washed my face and attempted to tame my hair. By the time I emerged, Alex was dressed and sitting on the sofa.

"Just give me another minute to change my clothes and then I'll be ready to go," I called out as I went to my room, shut the door, and closed my eyes so I could undress without worrying about Sebastian.

I quickly put on a pair of black jeans and a long-sleeved, slinky royal blue top with a moderately daring scoop-neck collar. I wasn't exactly well endowed, but the shirt definitely accentuated the positive. The push-up bra from Victoria's Secret helped, too. I finished the outfit with a pair of short, black leather boots and, as I surveyed myself in the mirror, was satisfied with the results. I transformed myself from average to ... approaching close to above average.

I walked into the living room to find Alex tossing an empty toilet paper roll for Vinnie to play with. The cat enthusiastically batted the cardboard tube around the floor and pounced on the tormenting cylinder before flopping on his side and rending it mercilessly with his back paws. Vinnie's amusing antics helped dispel any of my lingering mother-induced tension.

Alex looked up, smiled, and walked over to me. He leaned in before gently brushing his fingers against my hair, which was loose with curls cascading down my shoulders. My mother's call left me no time to straighten it.

"You look great," he murmured as our eyes met. "I like your hair this way."

Alex and I stared at each other for a moment. Gazing into those bright blue depths made me contemplate what it would be like to kiss him. His lips parted slightly and his mouth curved into another smile, smaller than the one before, but filled with much more heat.

Suddenly, all the seductive feelings fell away and I wanted to put as much distance between us as possible. Rather than giving in to my first inclination—to barricade myself in my room and escape into the desert by climbing out the window—I smiled back and said, "Thanks. We should get going, or we will be late," and then scooted away toward the front door.

Alex stood there for a bit, looking pensive and a little confused. He finally sighed, grabbed his jacket, and followed me outside.

We decided to take one car, figuring no one would be too suspicious if we carpooled downtown together. Alex drove, and on the way, he asked casually about the obviously strained relationship with my mother.

"She's a closed-minded, self-absorbed, religious fanatic who believes the earth was created six thousand years ago. What's not to love?" I began derisively. "She can never say anything nice and complains constantly. If I thought I could cut all contact and avoid being wracked with guilt, I would do it in a nanosecond."

"Human attachments are confusing to me," he said. "We try to distance ourselves from associations that are painful or negative, even familial relationships. But here, people stick to even the most destructive alliances, particularly when it comes to their parents."

I looked out the window into the night sky. The air was crisp and clear, and I could easily see hundreds of stars twinkling over the quiet desert.

"Hey, I don't get it either. My sisters found a way to have as little to do with her as possible, but it seems… I don't know… mean. I'm just happy I live many states away and only speak to her every few weeks. I feel bad for my father, though. I don't know how he stands it." I thought more carefully about what Alex had said and added, "The Coursodon probably don't tolerate bad relationships because they live so long. A couple hundred years is a long time to put up with someone's bullshit."

"Perhaps, but it would seem with a limited life span, one would be less likely to waste any of it with bullshit."

***

Luckily, when we arrived downtown, we found a parking spot just a block from the restaurant. Cafe Sin Vacas was tucked between an upscale tattoo parlor and a store that sold Native American jewelry. The place was decorated in minimalist-loft style: rough hardwood floors, exposed pipes, and raw brick walls filled with stainless-steel tables and chairs. Rachel and Harrison were already seated, and they waved us over when we entered.

Rachel, as always, looked fantastic. She wore a sea-green, V-necked cashmere sweater, with a tight, cream-colored leather miniskirt. Her shoes were the fashionable, high-heeled variety that I could never bring myself to spend the money on, much less be able to walk in. Harrison was his usual hot self—tall and muscular, his short, auburn hair accentuating his chiseled jaw and dark blue eyes.

Harrison rose as we approached and I introduced him to Alex. After their obligatory hand shake, Alex and I sat down next to each other, across from our dining companions. The waiter came by and asked what we wanted to drink and by the time the guys' beers and our margaritas arrived, Chelsea and Daniel had joined us.

Everyone was in a good mood, and the excellent meal and great company helped to make the evening fun and carefree. The menu, which changed daily based on the whims of the chef, was written on easel-propped blackboards that the wait staff brought to the tables. We all opted for the "Daily Special", which consisted of the chef's choice of three menu items. When the food arrived, none of us had the same selections, which allowed us to sample the entire delicious menu.

As we lingered over coffee, I couldn't help but notice the comfortable, affectionate familiarity the actual couples had settled into: Harrison brushed a stray wisp of hair behind Rachel's ear while she debated with Alex on the pros and cons of a two-party political system, and Chelsea leaned her head on Daniel's shoulder while they shared a piece of raspberry cheesecake. I wondered what it might be like to share that kind of closeness.

When it was time to pay the check, I assumed that we would split it such that the couples each paid a third, and Alex and I would be responsible for our own sixths—but when the bill arrived, Alex insisted on paying for both of us. At first, that seemed to indicate that he was viewing the evening as a date, which made me both giddy and uneasy. Soon, the more rational-me kicked in and I figured he was just trying to even things up for staying at my place.

As we got up to leave, Rachel leaned over to grab her purse, which she had set on the floor between our seats. Her position afforded me a birds-eye view of her ample cleavage, a panorama that drew a muffled groan from Sebastian. He'd remained delightfully silent through dinner, but his reaction sparked my mischievous side.

Time for some payback, Kess.

When Rachel stood, I allowed her to go ahead of me. I stayed put, though, making certain Sebastian got a good look at her as she sashayed toward the door. Alex, apparently confused by my delay, turned to see what was keeping me. He glanced first at me—my arms crossed and a wicked smile on my face—then at Rachel's shapely derriere, resplendent in the form-fitting leather that left little to the imagination. He lifted one eyebrow and a crooked smile swept across his lips. When I finally walked by, he shook his head slowly and snickered, "You are a cruel, cruel woman Ms. Parrish."

I nodded in agreement, Sebastian's deep voice echoing in my head.

"One hundred, ninety-three, eighty-six ..."

I nodded in agreement as I heard *"one hundred, ninety-three, eighty-six...,"* echoing in my head.

~9~

I was still laughing when Alex and I got to the car, thrilled to have finally settled the score with Sebastian. Well, to be honest, I made the score a little closer. Okay, I managed to prevent a shutout. Regardless of the magnitude of the triumph, at least for a moment, I felt I had some control over my situation.

Just before we pulled away from the curb, Alex's phone rang. The ensuing conversation was short and one-sided, with Alex supplying only an occasional "Yes" or "Uh-huh." He disconnected, and said, "That was one of my contacts. He has a lead on someone that might know what happened to Sebastian's body."

"That's great," I replied. "Finally, some progress."

"Yes, and the best part is, we won't have to go far to meet up with this guy." Alex placed his palm over mine. "Sebastian, do you remember Xu Tao?"

"The pearl dealer from Hong Kong? I remember him well. His reputation as an informant is unmatched."

Alex continued speaking out loud, so I could participate in the conversation. "He is willing to divulge what he knows about your corporeal-self. Luckily, he will be here, in Tucson, next week for the Gem Show."

The annual Gem and Mineral Showcase was a world-renowned, international marketplace where fifty-thousand people invaded Tucson to buy and sell anything from jewelry to fossils. For two weeks at the end of January and beginning of February, shows were staged all over town in hotels, meeting halls, and even huge tents erected just for the event. I had never actually been to any of the shows, but I knew all about it because each year the local media was dominated with its coverage. Plus, all the good restaurants were packed.

"That is indeed fortuitous," Sebastian intoned, *"both for the likely usefulness of the information to be gained as well as the lack of travel required."*

As usual, I felt as if I was missing something. "How does a guy who exports pearls have the inside scoop on a nefarious, other-worldly crime boss?"

"It is not uncommon in both our dimensions to have legitimate enterprises that benefit from contact with shadier elements. Kashanian's syndicate guarantees, for a cut of the profits, that Mr. Xu's pearls move safely from production to distribution. And Mr. Xu finds he can supplement his already prodigious earnings by keeping his eyes and ears open and doing business with both sides," Sebastian explained.

"I guess that's one way to even up the cost of extortion."

"Not precisely extortion, my dear, but what he makes as a snitch hardly compensates for the amount he loses. But, I suspect it soothes the sting a bit to be able to stick it to Kashanian, even if only in some small way."

"So, does Xu know Kashanian, or you guys for that matter, aren't human?" I asked.

"Of course," Alex chimed in. "Xu's not completely human either. His father was Courso and his mother was human."

I had no idea there were supernatural mixed marriages. And I thought it was a problem that my father was a Red Sox fan and my mom rooted for the Yankees.

"That explains the 'why', but wouldn't it be easier and faster if he just called or emailed the information?"

Alex nodded. "For us, yes. But Mr. Xu only exchanges knowledge for money, and he doesn't take credit cards."

I obviously had a lot to learn about the seedier side of life, but it made sense that Xu would want to meet face to face. This was certainly a positive development, in any case. Finally, we were making some headway into restoring Sebastian to his own body. Of course, as soon as we accomplished the deconvergence, or whatever the proper term was, Alex would have no reason to remain here.

This was so typical. I wanted nothing more than to be the sole occupant of my body, but at the same time, the thought of Alex leaving bummed me out. Not only was he great to be around, but really, the whole supernatural-magical-parallel dimension business was much more exciting than my normal life.

Alex removed his hand from mine and started driving. After a few minutes, he glanced at me and smiled, then turned back to concentrate on the road.

"I had a good time tonight."

"Me too," I confessed. Suddenly feeling a bit uncomfortable, I added, "As non-dates go, this one was one of the best."

He laughed. "Wow, high praise indeed. What makes this not a date?"

I paused to consider my answer. "Well, for one thing, we all decided to go out together. You didn't specifically ask me out."

"True. But we did arrive and leave together."

It was dark in the car, so he couldn't see my expression, but my tone conveyed my skepticism.

"It takes more than shared transportation to constitute a date, Alex. Using your logic, I've been on about two hundred of them with Rachel."

"Okay," he continued playfully. "But I did pay for dinner."

I sighed with mock exasperation. "There you go again, making spurious correlations. If you recall, I offered to pay my share, but you wouldn't let me. Again, I think everything points to non-date."

He laughed again. "There are no spurious correlations, only spurious interpretations. But you are quite persuasive, so I suppose I will have to concede that this was not an actual date."

I'd won the argument, but the victory seemed hollow. *What the hell was I thinking?* I was with a sexy, intelligent, handsome guy and while trying to keep things breezy, I succeed in convincing him that this was nothing but a casual get-together. Which it probably really was and he was just joking. Or not. *Crap.* Now I felt like I was fifteen again, not thirty. Maybe I could pass him a note after homeroom.

I figured I had already backed myself into a corner, and decided to keep the light-hearted theme going.

"Well, if it makes you feel better, this was by far the very best non-date, with a non-human, I've ever been on."

"It does, and date or not, I still get to go home with you. I think that counts for something."

"If he was as smart as he thinks," the little voice inside me piped in, *"it would count for everything."*

***

The show Xu attended didn't open until Thursday. Even though he'd be in town a couple of days before that, the pearl dealer insisted that the meeting take place in the anonymity afforded by the crowded venue. While it seemed to me that these types of things were best suited to dark alleys or smoke-filled taverns in out of the way places, Alex and Sebastian assured me that this made more sense. If anyone noticed us talking in such a public place, who would suspect anything other than commerce was going on? I could see the logic, but had to admit it was a little disappointing that rather than cloak and dagger, this was going to be more like show and tell.

In the meantime, I played tour guide so Alex and Sebastian could take in some of the sites around the area. On Saturday, we went to the Arizona Sonora Desert Museum and spent almost the entire day there. The Desert Museum was more zoo than anything, housing all sorts of plants and animals—from mountain lions to tiny elf owls—that could be found in the surrounding desert, presented in a natural, peaceful setting.

Alex was particularly enamored with an eight-inch-long, giant desert centipede, a truly hideous creature with a segmented body and lots of pointy legs. I could barely look at the thing, but he wanted to count the legs to see if there really were a hundred. Apparently, the other dimension is devoid of such grotesque insect life—a big plus in my book, by the way—which made it even more fascinating to Alex. Sebastian couldn't understand why I was so squeamish, and delighted in torturing me with graphic details of what it must be like to have one crawl up your arm or find one in your bed. Although I had never seen one in the wild, before I went to sleep that night, I pulled back all the covers and shined a flashlight over and under my bed, just to be on the safe side.

I arranged the schedule at work so that it wouldn't be a problem for me to take Thursday off and then figured, what the hell, I hadn't taken any vacation time in a while and planned on not going in on Friday either. Chelsea and Rachel jokingly complained about how the minions are always the ones who suffer when management slacks off, but I knew they didn't really mind me having a long weekend.

Of course, once they heard that Alex wouldn't be at work either, they were convinced that we were going off together on a romantic getaway. It was obvious that they wanted to press for specifics, but Alex was always around whenever they had an opportunity to ask. As I couldn't begin to explain what we were really planning, I figured it was easier to let them assume I was finally going to get some. Besides, if we figured out where Sebastian's body was, I'd have to take a lot more time off to go to China. Fortunately, I already had a passport for those occasional trips down to Rocky Point to enjoy the Mexican beaches—that was one detail I didn't have to worry about.

On Thursday, Alex and I went to meet Xu at a hotel near the airport that hosted one of the bigger shows. There were some merchants in the ballroom and lobby, but most of the vendors bought booth space in massive, connecting tents set up in the parking lot.

As this was a wholesale event, only those with business licenses could attend. Alex had somehow secured the proper credentials for us to enter, handing me an ID badge. We were now buyers for *Running with Scissors Jewelry Designs*, located in Moose Jaw, Saskatchewan. I was about to ask if either the business or the town existed, but as we walked through the front entrance, the controlled mayhem before me made me lose my train of thought.

The football field-sized tent was packed with row after row of tables, racks, and displays bursting with anything anyone might need to create personal adornments. Most of the really expensive stuff—diamonds and pre-made gold and platinum jewelry—was protected in glass cases. However, bowls filled with faceted and cut rubies, sapphires, and emeralds were just sitting on tables, much like how one might put out M&Ms for a party. Strands of sparkling, semi-precious beads hung like Christmas lights from pegboard walls temporarily erected to exhibit the wares. In booth after booth, the scene was repeated hundreds of times in an overwhelming hodgepodge of colors, shapes, and textures. The multitude of languages people were speaking, most of which I could not identify, only added to my sense of wonder.

The aisles were crowded with buyers perusing the merchandise and armed law enforcement personnel were posted at each exit. That made sense—the combined worth of everything in the tents were probably more than the GNP of many a small nation. While Alex figured out where Xu's booth was located, I watched in fascination as a man handed over five grand in cash to purchase Australian opals, all of which fit into a tiny, plastic zip-top bag that he stuffed into his shirt pocket.

Even with his mixed heritage, because Xu knew Sebastian well, he would likely be able to sense Sebastian's essence in me. Although the pearl merchant might not completely understand what was going on, he was a notorious conniver and couldn't be trusted not to divulge the information to someone for the right price. Alex explained that as long as he and I stayed in physical contact, he could mask Sebastian's essence. It wasn't possible to eliminate all traces of magic, so Xu would believe that I, too, was Courso, but at least Sebastian's spiritual disembodiment would not be discovered.

Alex motioned to me to follow, and I noticed that as we made our way toward the back of the second tent, he gave a small nod to a vendor or two along the way.

"Do you know those guys?" I questioned, surprised that he might be acquainted with anyone here.

"I don't know them personally," he replied, "but the Coursodon have dominated the bead and pearl trade for centuries. We can sense each other's magical signatures and it's considered impolite not to acknowledge a fellow Courso. You should probably do the same."

I had forgotten that I was sending out other-worldly vibes and wasn't aware that we would be around any Coursodon other than Xu.

"Why would people with magical abilities be drawn to this particular industry?"

He stopped and pointed to a strand of impossibly small tanzanite beads, each not even as large as the head of a pin.

"Do you think someone without magic could make all the teeny, tiny little holes in these things?"

Xu's spot was larger than most, taking up the equivalent of four or five of the average booths. There were tables surrounding the perimeter, with two small openings to allow passage into the interior, which was filled with more tables. Every inch of space was covered with mounds of pearls strung on individual, sixteen-inch strands bunched in larger groups of like-strands called hanks. Round ones, square ones, pearls shaped like buttons or corn flakes, most were natural shades of white, cream, or gray, but some were dyed in every color of the rainbow. As varied and plentiful as were Xu's offerings, twenty other merchants throughout the building were selling the same merchandise.

Alex grabbed my hand and navigated through the maze of tables toward an Asian-appearing fellow perched on a small stool in the center of the display. Xu stood as we approached, and inclined his head slightly in greeting.

He was a good three inches shorter than my five-foot-six, but what he lacked in height, he made up for in girth. His massive rolls of pale, corpulent flesh reminded me of a melting candle, and if not for the presence of stubby legs, Xu would have been a dead ringer for Jabba the Hutt.

"He is quite the looker, is he not?" Sebastian noted.

I suppressed a giggle but Alex gave my hand a slight squeeze as a reminder to ignore the sarcasm.

"Mr. Xu," he said. "How nice to see you again."

Alex didn't really seem pleased. In fact, between the scowl on his face and tone in his voice, I could practically feel the animosity.

"I don't believe I have had the privilege of making the acquaintance of your lovely companion," Xu remarked obsequiously, fingering a tray of black Tahitian pearls next to him.

"No, you have not," was Alex's only reply.

They stared at each other for a moment and once Xu realized that that was the extent of our introduction, he waddled past us and picked up a hank of pearls.

"I set these aside just for you. I believe this is what you requested."

"The quality appears to be excellent, as usual." Alex made a show of examining each strand closely. "However, I was looking for more conformity in size and shape."

"Perhaps I have something more to your liking in the back." Xu led us to the far end of the booth and began spreading out more trays of pearls. "Of course, one can always be assured of satisfaction when dealing with me," he responded emphatically, emphasizing the word "satisfaction" while ogling my chest.

"I suppose, for him, that is the only satisfaction he can expect from a woman. He is so obese he likely has not seen his own penis in decades."

Feigning a cough to disguise my laughter, I noticed a slight quiver of Alex's lips as he, too, must have found Sebastian's comment amusing. Ever the professional, however, he recovered quickly. "Let's get down to business, shall we?"

Xu leaned in, lowering his voice while he continued the affectations of salesmanship. "The body is not in China," he began. "Otto had it transported somewhere else."

Alex frowned. "Transported? Where?"

Xu placed a few strands of pearls into a small paper bag before answering.

"It is purported that it was taken to one of Kashanian's many residences throughout the world, but I was unable to determine which one."

"Why would he take the body?" I interrupted. Both Alex and Xu looked at me as if they were surprised I could actually speak, and I wondered if I was missing something obvious. Somewhat embarrassed, but not knowing exactly why, I pressed on in an attempt to appear knowledgeable about what one usually does with the remains of someone they murdered. "Why not just leave it where it was?"

"I have no solid information, but speculation is that he is retaining it as a sort of trophy to commemorate his victory over the great Sebastian," Xu said with a shrug and a nasty smile.

Alex and I stared at the rotund pearl dealer, then glanced at each other. Sebastian had no comment about the possibility that his body was being displayed somewhere for Otto's amusement, but I was appalled. *Otto Kashanian must be one sick bastard.* It was bad enough he had no problem offing someone, but keeping the body as a souvenir was downright gruesome.

Alex frowned again. After a moment, he reached into his pocket and withdrew a large wad of hundred-dollar bills, which he passed to Xu in exchange for the bag. Then we left the booth.

When we were a few aisles away, Sebastian let loose with a litany of expletives, some of which described things that I was sure were physically impossible, even for someone magically inclined or really flexible.

Eventually, he calmed enough to limit his remarks to how he planned to get back at Otto, all of which ended with Otto being tortured, dead, or both.

Listening to Sebastian's revenge schemes gave me a headache, so I tried to direct the conversation in a more constructive direction.

"So, if Xu's information is correct, why would Otto transport the body out of China?"

"I'm also surprised he would go to so much trouble," Alex replied. "At least we know why no one found a body where Sebastian was attacked."

We walked around for a while, stopping at various booths, trying to look like buyers. Alex even purchased a few additional strands of beads to complete the ruse, and after about an hour, we made our way back to the car.

As Alex maneuvered out of the crowded parking lot, I pulled a strand of Xu's pearls out of the bag for a closer look. "These are pretty, but they aren't really worth what you paid for them, right?"

He glanced over at the strand I was examining. "That's probably one-hundred dollars' worth of mollusk spit for which I handed over ten-thousand. If his information is correct, it was worth the price."

"Ten-thousand dollars?" I sputtered. "He didn't even know exactly where the body is located."

Alex took one hand off the steering wheel, reached over, and took hold of mine. "If he had that information, I would have gladly given him much more. As it is, knowing that Otto plans to retain Sebastian's body as a memento will help us to recover it."

"And force that loathsome barbarian to watch while I rip out one of his eyes and feed it to a stray dog!"

I wasn't positive that a dog would eat someone's eye, but I wasn't about to argue the point with Sebastian. Instead, I settled for, "Gross."

"That image disturbs you, my dear? You should be thankful I did not go with my first choice—cutting off his dick and fucking him with it."

"Sebastian," Alex chided. He could hear the tirade because he was still holding my hand. "That's enough. What Otto has done is reprehensible, but let's try to focus on finding where he has your body. Besides, I am quite certain that someone's penis, once removed from their body, would be unsuitable for the task you intend."

"Wow, Sebastian," I muttered. "I had no idea you were such a bad ass."

"Did you think I was the most feared Xyzok of the last century because of my acerbic wit?"

Truthfully, I hadn't really thought about him in any way other than just being a pain in my butt. Or, in my head at the moment. A somewhat amusing one to be sure, but I never really considered that in his line of work, he must be damn tough.

"Uh, sorry. It's just you always seem so, I don't know, controlled, I suppose. It's kind of shocking to hear you go off like that. And a little scary."

"I apologize for frightening you, but I am outraged that scum like Kashanian would use my corporeal being in such a manner."

"Keeping your body is quite unusual," Alex agreed. "And fraught with a variety of logistical complications, I would imagine. But now we need to focus on figuring out where he has you stashed."

The rest of the drive back to my place, Alex and Sebastian bounced ideas off one another and ultimately decided, once they researched all Kashanian's known residences, the options could likely be narrowed to the one or two locations. Their criteria for what constituted these standout locales was a bit fuzzy to me, but they seemed certain there would be an obvious choice. After all, they did this kind of thing for a living; they must know what they were doing. My unease was growing, however. After Sebastian's venomous rant, what had originally seemed like an adventure might be more dangerous than I had imagined.

~10~

As soon as we got back to the house, Alex booted up his laptop and got to work finding Otto's hideouts. I watched over his shoulder as he used what seemed to be not completely legal backdoors to maneuver through the morass of records littered with aliases and false paper trails. He was already aware of one residence in Vanuatu and another in Iceland, but within a couple of hours, he identified an additional six places throughout the world that Otto called home.

While Alex embarked on the next phase of his sleuthing—trying to determine if, on the day in question, any private jets traveled between Shenzhen to any of the eight places where Otto owned property—I absentmindedly glanced at the list.

"What if Otto brought Sebastian's body to your dimension, and he's not at any of these places?" I asked.

Without looking away from the screen or slowing his astonishingly rapid typing on the keyboard, Alex answered. "Luckily for us, a Courso body cannot be moved from one dimension to another. The lack of the magical essence renders the empty corporeal shell nontransferable. He would have to keep the body in the dimension where the deconvergence occurred."

"How do you know that? I thought this was the first time anyone had been deconverged."

"This is the first time anyone has accomplished deconvergence in a controlled manner," Sebastian explained. *"Technically speaking, any time a Courso dies and his or her spiritual-self separates from their body, deconvergence occurs. That's how we know an empty body is not able to be transported."*

"What happens if someone tried it; does the body hit an invisible wall or something?"

"That is what happens if a human tried to cross from one dimension to another. An empty Courso body would disintegrate."

"Oh, so it's not that it *can't* move to the other dimension, it just can't move *intact*," I reasoned.

Alex, who had apparently deduced Sebastian's comments from my responses, paused from his work and added, "That's why we strongly believe Sebastian's body is still in this dimension. Why would Kashanian go to all the trouble to commandeer it only to let it be obliterated?"

That seemed a sensible conclusion, but this whole business seemed so bizarre, I wasn't sure if there was truly any logic involved.

Alex continued to work into the evening, only slowing slightly when I brought him a sandwich for dinner. I kept myself busy with mundane tasks around the guesthouse; I wanted to go out and run some errands, but stuck around in case Alex needed to confer with Sebastian.

Around nine o'clock, after I finished organizing my sock drawer for the second time, I went into the living room to check on Alex's progress. He wasn't at the computer, and a glance around made it clear he wasn't inside at all.

I went to the sliding glass door and looked out. Even without turning on the light, the full moon illuminated the patio. There was Alex, head thrown back and his eyes closed, leaning against the short adobe wall that surrounded the flagstone porch.

I grabbed a sweater and stepped outside as quietly as possible, not wanting to startle him from his serene pose.

He didn't move, but acknowledged my presence with a soft, "It's such a beautiful night, I thought I'd take a break out here."

It was beautiful, although a bit chilly for my taste, even with the added layer.

"You want some company?"

Alex turned around and offered one of his mega-smiles. "Sure. No sense wasting all this on just me."

As I moved to stand next to him, he resumed his former stance.

"You know, you kind of look like you're basking in the sun right now," I noted.

He opened his eyes and regarded me. "That's an apt analogy. We get our vitamin D through moonlight, so I was making good use of the clear skies and the favorable lunar phase."

I thought about that for a minute, trying to reconcile my knowledge of human physiology with this new tidbit. "Does sunlight stimulate production of too much vitamin D for you?"

"Partly, but synthesis of our vitamin D doesn't require ultraviolet wavelengths, either. Before the advent of sunscreen with high SPFs, we were forced to cover ourselves during daylight hours."

I stared at him for a moment. "You seem so human, but there's obviously a lot that's different between us. I'd love to get a look at a Coursodon physiology textbook."

"When I get a chance, I'll try and locate such a book and you can research whatever you like. But it will all be written in Courso, so I guess it won't really be that useful to you."

"Can't I just surf the net and look at the pictures?" I jested.

"Our Internet can't be accessed from this dimension, nor can yours from ours. The same with other means of communication, like cell phones or radio." He paused for a moment. "I suppose that someone very clever could figure out a way to bridge the dimensions, but compared to your human advances in such areas, ours are rather primitive. The Courso tend to shy away from technology in favor of magic."

I shook my head. "There it is again. It makes sense that another dimension would have their own technologies not accessible to us. I just never considered all the possible ramifications of the existence of more than one world. I couldn't figure it all out even if I spent the rest of my life researching."

As my last comment left my lips, I remembered that humans weren't really supposed to know about Coursodon. "Of course, whatever I know will only be for my benefit. I would never tell anyone about you."

Alex turned to face me again. "I am quite certain that you would not betray our trust." Then his serious expression gave way to a small, teasing smile and he added, "If you did, I can always erase your memory after all this is over."

"Erase my memory? You can do that?"

He laughed and put his arm around my shoulder. "Don't worry, Hailey. I could do it, but I wouldn't."

I looked up at him with some skepticism, but upon further consideration, figured if he was planning on something that dastardly, he certainly wouldn't tell me about it. Only in poorly written fiction did the bad guys reveal their evil intentions before carrying them out.

"You know," I joked, "between the moonlight and your ability to alter someone's mind, you could be a vampire."

"It's interesting that you should make that association. We believe that many of the legends about vampires, werewolves, and various other supernatural creatures are tales of interactions between humans and Courso. Particularly because until relatively recently, the only Coursodon that made their way to this dimension were the dregs of our society. We are stronger and faster than humans, and all our senses, with the exception of taste, are much more acute than yours. It is also possible for some of us to alter our appearance. Three or four hundred years ago, if you saw someone with magical abilities that was also capable of great violence, you would create stories of all sorts of nasty monsters to explain it."

"Courso can change themselves into animals?"

"Not everyone. It takes a tremendous amount of energy and focus, so it's not something that can be easily achieved. Even those with extremely well-developed magical ability can accomplish form change for only short periods of time. And it takes a long time to recover."

I tried to imagine fiendish Courso, exiled to our world, satisfying their vicious, antisocial tendencies in ways that would evolve into legends of people transforming into wolves or feasting on human blood.

I quickly abandoned this grisly train of thought and realized that Alex's arm was still draped across my shoulders. Even though the logical part of me enjoyed the contact, the inner, irrational me was freaking out at the prospect of this going any further.

Unfortunately, freaked Hailey won out and I slipped out from under his arm, retreating to one of the lounge chairs. Rational Hailey thought it was a fairly slick move, but apparently, it didn't fool Alex.

He observed me thoughtfully for a minute or so, and then sat down in the chair next to mine.

"I know I've insinuated myself into your life because of very unusual circumstances, but I get the feeling you still don't completely trust me. Maybe we haven't known each other long enough for me to have earned your trust, but I want that more than you can imagine."

I peered out into the desert that surrounded the property, noting the shadows of the saguaro cactus being cast by the moonlight. I briefly considered trying to avoid the conversation by fleeing into the spiny forest, but figured it was time to woman-up and explain my wariness.

"It's not that I don't trust *you*," I began. "I have a problem trusting men in general."

"You want to tell me about it?"

I definitely did not want to discuss my neuroses, but decided he deserved an explanation. Besides, if I didn't tell him, he could just ask Rachel why I seemed so twitchy when it came to the opposite sex.

While continuing to focus on the shadowy landscape before me, I began my tale of woe.

"I was married to Kyle for almost a year. We met while I was finishing grad school and he was in law school. I thought he was fantastic—handsome, intelligent—and was amazed that he was interested in me. We were both busy with classes, but dated for six months before deciding we couldn't live without each other and eloped. I thought everything was great until a new technician started working in the lab where I was getting my master's. On her first day, everyone in the lab was sitting around waiting for a meeting to start, and she started talking about her law-student boyfriend. She kept going on and on about *Kyle* this and *Kyle* that, and it became apparent that her boyfriend was my husband. I hadn't taken his last name, so there was no way she would have known.

"It was bad enough finding out my marriage was a sham, but to be told in front of the people I worked with made it all the more humiliating. My co-workers tried to get one of us out of the room, or at least get her to shut up, but I kept asking questions. Turned out, they had been together for almost the entire time we were married. When Kyle said he was studying late at night, or on weekends, he was with her and I was too stupid to figure it out. I should have known anyone who studied that much should have better grades."

I finally glanced over and saw that Alex looked like he had just eaten something extremely distasteful, like expired sushi or chitlins. "That's horrible," he muttered. "What are the odds of the two of you working at the same place?"

"I know, if it hadn't actually happened to me, I would think it was something that could only occur in a made-for-TV movie."

"What happened when you confronted him?"

"He didn't seem all that upset that I knew, or over how I found out. I moved out that day and filed for divorce the day after that."

Alex shook his head slowly. "How did you handle the work situation?"

"The woman had no idea Kyle was married and broke up with him. Mortified about what happened—both the affair itself and the manner in which Kyle's infidelity was exposed—she quit the same afternoon. She lost a job and a man in less than twenty-four hours."

We sat there for a few moments before Alex broke the awkward silence. "I feel like a complete cad. Please, please, forgive my insensitivity. Here I am, telling you that you should trust me, and I make you re-live what must have been the worst day of your life."

His unabashed contrition was actually kind of endearing, and I felt bad that he felt so bad. "It's okay, Alex, really," I said, leaning towards him to place my hand over his. "The way it went down definitely sucked, but obviously it was never a good relationship—no matter how much I may have wanted it to be. Rachel hated Kyle the minute she met him. There were warning signs, even before we got married that I should have paid more attention to, but I think I was just in love with being in love, rather than actually being in love with him."

Alex rotated his palm so he could squeeze my hand. "You deserve so much more, Hailey."

"Thanks. You know, if it would make you feel better, I'll tell you where he lives and you can turn him into one of those nasty centipedes you liked so much."

"That, my dear, would be far too good for the likes of that cretin," Sebastian offered. He he'd been so quiet, I'd almost forgotten he was there.

Alex nodded his head in agreement. "Good point, my friend. I say we wait until you're reconverged and then you can do what you planned for Kashanian."

Sebastian responded with a small chuckle. *"Which, the eye thing or the dick thing?"*

"Oh, definitely the dick thing," I quipped.

Alex's eyes widened and then he threw back his head and laughed, long and hard. When he finished, he crossed his arms and said with mock indignation, "I thought you found Sebastian's revenge scenarios disturbing, and here you are embracing them when it suits your own purposes."

"Yeah, well, a girl has a right to change her mind."

Raising an eyebrow, Alex shot me a skeptical look. "Remind me never to make you mad."

"I rather like the vindictive, implacable side of you, my dear. I believe there is hope for you yet."

The discussion of my ersatz marriage was exhausting, and now that I'd bared my soul—or at least my relationship failures—to Alex, there didn't seem to be much more to talk about. He abandoned the moon-bathing and went back to trying to determine where Otto stashed Sebastian's body, and I went to bed.

The next day brought a number of promising leads, but no definitive answers about where Kashanian had transported the body. By dinnertime, it was apparent that Alex needed a break, so we drove over to O'Reilly's.

We arrived during the lull between when the happy hour crowd drifted off and the Friday night music lovers showed up and had our choice of tables. I waved at Wyatt when we sat down and could have sworn he smirked when he saw me with Alex. I preferred to believe that Wyatt was just giving me props for hooking up with a hot guy rather than the more likely explanation that he was surprised I was with any guy.

I ordered the blue cheese burger—medium rare—to appease Sebastian, while Alex opted for a healthier grilled chicken sandwich with green chilies. On the drive to

O'Reilly's, we decided to avoid discussing our "mission" while at dinner, so the conversation remained supremely low key and pleasant.

Rejuvenated by the influx of carbs and grease, we drove home and returned to the task at hand. By Monday morning, Alex had eliminated three of Kashanian's residences, but the process was slow and tedious because, let's face it, criminals don't generally feel compelled to conform to regulations like filing flight plans. That meant Alex had to use other, more circuitous means to ascertain where Sebastian had been taken.

When I got back from work, he had determined that a plane, likely belonging to Kashanian, had taken off the morning after Sebastian was attacked, made a short refueling stop at a small airport in northern India, then continued on to another out-of-the-way airport outside of Ankara, Turkey. The plane remained there for a day, during which time another jet arrived. Each jet then traveled to different locales—one to the Czech Republic, the other to Tunisia—near where Otto had homes.

While we were in the middle of a discussion about the two possibilities, my cell phone rang. I didn't recognize the number and when I answered, was surprised when the unknown caller identified himself as Wyatt, from O'Reilly's.

I knew Wyatt had never called me before, in fact, I was pretty sure I had never spoken to him outside of the bar. My bewilderment regarding the situation must have been readily apparent, because Alex furrowed his brow and mouthed, "Everything okay?"

I shrugged, and asked Wyatt what was up.

"There was a guy in here earlier asking questions about you," he explained. "Not by name, but he described you and showed me a photo of that tall, blond dude you were in here with."

That didn't sound good. "What did he want to know?"

"Like, how often you came in, where you work. Oh, and if I'd known you for a long time," he added. "It was weird. He introduced himself as Detective something, and handed me a fake law enforcement ID."

"How did you know it was fake?" I asked.

"I'm a bartender. I see fake crap all the time, and frankly, sixteen-year-olds trying to get served have more believable shit than this jerk offered."

I was starting to feel a little queasy, so I sat down on the sofa and took a deep breath before I continued.

"What did you tell him?"

"Nothing. I said I didn't recognize the guy in the picture and I had no idea who the woman he described was either. You need to be careful, Hailey. I don't know what the deal is with this phony cop or the guy you're hanging with, but I wanted to give you a heads up."

"Ask him for a description," Sebastian whispered in my head.

"What did this detective look like?"

"About five-foot-nine or ten, I'd guess. Big guns, looks like he's pretty serious about bodybuilding—short, dark hair, and a tat on his left hand, some sort of a squiggly design. Sound familiar?"

"Not at all," I replied. "Hey, thanks Wyatt. I appreciate you letting me know about this." I was about to say goodbye when I realized another question needed answering. "By the way, how did you get my number?"

"Men's bathroom, second stall," he stated, matter-of-factly.

"Excuse me?"

"Just trying to lighten the mood," he confessed, chortling softly. "One of the dishwashers knows Chelsea, so I had him get it from her. But seriously, girl, watch your back."

I ended the call and relayed the information to Alex. He immediately reached over, took my hand and conferred with Sebastian on these new and troubling developments, but, whatever his motivation, I was happy for the contact. Knowing that someone—probably a not nice someone—was poking around my life was not a development I was prepared for.

I leaned my head onto the back of the sofa and tried to relax by telling myself that I was probably making a bigger deal about this than was warranted. Unfortunately, listening to Alex and Sebastian wasn't making me feel any calmer.

"I don't like this," Alex grumbled. "It can't be a coincidence that we get some actionable intel from Xu and within a few days, someone is asking questions about Hailey and me."

"Xu is many things, most of which are despicable, but he values his ties to both sides too much to jeopardize himself with a double-cross. Besides, even if he did tell Otto that you had been asking about me, why would Otto go to the trouble of sending someone here?"

Alex hesitated a moment, seemingly deep in thought, before he answered. "Right now, it doesn't matter who or why. I'm more concerned about making sure that Hailey is in no danger. We need to move somewhere safer, and we need to do it now."

Yep, this is exactly what I was trying to convince myself wasn't an inevitable problem with having low-lives snooping around, asking for information. I glanced at Alex, who took both my hands in his before declaring, "I'm so sorry about this, but I think the wisest course is to leave here as soon as possible. I need to make some arrangements; can you pack a few things to get ready?"

I nodded and stood up, pleased that I was able to accomplish the latter without my knees knocking. As I turned to go into my room to figure out what one packs to go into hiding, Vinnie meandered across the living room and plunked himself down in the middle of the floor. I'd have to call Rachel and make sure she could watch him while I was gone. And work… shit, what was I going to do about my job?

I realized that there was more to do than just throw some stuff in a bag before I could take off to wherever for however long this was going to take. I pulled in a deep breath and tried to think clearly. I still had a bunch of vacation time accrued, but no one was going to be happy with an unscheduled absence on short notice.

I turned back toward Alex, who was already talking to someone on his phone. He noticed me and finished his conversation shortly thereafter.

"We'll use a friend's place in New Hampshire," he said as he ended the call. "I just need to coordinate travel plans."

"What am I supposed to say to explain why I am suddenly leaving town?" I asked, much more frantically than I had intended. "I can't very well tell anyone the truth, but I have to come up with something at least vaguely credible. Any ideas, boys?"

After some discussion, we decided on a story: My sister Sarah was once again in a family way, but confined to bed due to complications. I was going to go to Ohio to help take care of my nieces while her husband, Terry, continued to run their dry-cleaning establishment. Rachel and Chelsea should find that believable, as Sarah had had some minor problems during her last pregnancy, and they knew enough about Terry to accept that he wouldn't be able to supervise a business and three children under the age of four by himself. A sticking point could be that I rarely spoke to, much less saw, any of my sisters, but if anyone wondered I'd just claim I wanted to get closer to my siblings. What better way to do so than helping out in this time of need?

That settled, I went to my room to pack. I had never been to New Hampshire before, but I assumed it would be cold this time of year. This posed a problem, considering my winter wardrobe of lightweight shirts and jeans probably wouldn't be adequate for the Great White North. While I searched through my closet for the few wintry clothing choices I owned, I called Rachel.

"Hey, Rach," I said when she answered. "I need a huge favor."

I explained my predicament, at least the fabricated one, and Rachel agreed to take care of Vinnie without hesitation.

"No problem, Hails. You want me to drop by to feed him and clean the litter?"

"Not a good idea. We cannot be certain that this miscreant will not discover where you live, and if he does, it will be safer for Rachel if she is not going in and out of your house."

Leave it to Sebastian to consider the worst-case scenario. I hadn't considered that the potential for danger here might continue once we were gone. The last thing I wanted was put anyone else in peril, particularly not my best friend or my cat.

"Actually, I'm not sure how long I will be gone. Hopefully, it'll just be a few days and Sarah and Terry can make other arrangements, but it could be as long as a week or two. Vinnie doesn't do well when he is alone; could I bring him to your house?"

I wasn't kidding about Vinnie's need for human companionship. Last year, I left him with food and water while I spent a weekend at the American Cheese Makers Association's annual convention in San Diego and he became uncharacteristically destructive.

"Good point. I don't want to have to relive the experience of helping you clean cat puke out of all your shoes. Bring him over," Rachel replied.

"Thanks, Rach, you're the best. I'll get his stuff together and drop him off in an hour or so."

"Sounds good. Besides, this will give me a chance to check out how Harrison acts with pets. I've heard that you can judge how a guy will be with kids by the way he acts with animals."

"Are you and Harrison talking about having children?"

Why their decision to conceive seemed inconceivable made no sense at all. Probably a deep-seated desire for some normalcy was the culprit, given all the abnormal shit currently happening in my life. Still, Rachel and Harrison becoming parents suggested more weirdness than I could handle.

Rachel huffed out an exasperated breath. "Calm down. We aren't at that point yet, but since I want to have a family someday, it never hurts to do a little investigation beforehand."

"Where did you hear that? I've known plenty of people who love animals but are a disaster with kids, and vice versa."

"I read that Maria Shriver's father gave her that advice about Arnold Schwarzenegger." Rachel declared. "Although, now that I think of it, that advice didn't work out so well for Maria and Arnold, did it?"

We finalized the details of Vinnie's care before I ended the call. Next, I phoned my boss, and lucked out when I got his answering machine. I left an appropriately contrite message, apologizing profusely for using my vacation time on such short notice, and assuring him that I had made the proper arrangements with the rest of the staff to provide full coverage while I was away.

Tasks completed, I inspected the mound of potential packables laid out on the bed. Jeans, a pair of sweatpants, a couple of long-sleeved tees, a flannel shirt, a fleece jacket, and a long-forgotten pullover sweater comprised the ragtag collection of items I assembled. I added underwear, socks, and some hiking boots. It wasn't high fashion, but at least I had enough layers to keep me from freezing. I hoped. Some essential toiletry items went into a small pouch which I tucked into the zippered pocket on the outside of the bag.

When I returned to the living room, Alex was absorbed in yet another call. This time, he was speaking a language so unlike any I had ever encountered—an odd mix of guttural sounds interspersed with bird-like trills—I assumed it must Courso. I listened carefully but was still unable to distinguish individual words. Although I couldn't understand what he was saying, the deep creases in Alex's brow strongly suggested he was not happy. When he finished, he leaned his head back and let out a long, deep breath. However, as I moved across his line of vision to deposit my bag near the front door, his bearing quickly changed back to his usual cheery calm.

"All packed?"

I briefly contemplated inquiring about what had him so troubled, but if he was making such an effort to keep me in the dark, I was probably better off not knowing the details. Instead, I simply remarked, "Yep, I just need to get Vinnie and his stuff together and we can get going."

"Don't forget your passport. You have one, yes?"

"Yes, but last time I checked, New Hampshire didn't require one for entry." I regretted the sarcasm immediately, particularly because of the frown it elicited from Alex.

"New Hampshire doesn't, but we have no idea if we will be traveling to other places where proof of citizenship is considered compulsory."

"Always best to be prepared for any contingency, my dear," Sebastian chimed in. *"Although, in truth, it would be best if you did not use anything with your real name. Perhaps we can have some forged documentation prepared for you instead."*

Wow. A counterfeit passport with a fictitious name was kind of exciting.

"Sebastian thinks I should have fake IDs."

"That's an excellent idea, Sebastian," he said, punching in a number on his phone. "I'll get Tannis on that right away."

While Alex waited for his call to be answered, I inquired if I could choose my own pseudonym. "Unfortunately, you can't," he advised. "On short notice, one takes whatever one can get."

I harrumphed in disappointment. Instead of being able to conjure up a cool name, like Tannis—whoever that was—I'd probably end up being Bertha Butz.

Once again, Alex spoke the same incomprehensible language, but instead of worry, this conversation brought about familiar ease. Even though I couldn't understand one word, Alex's demeanor, the lowered voice, and rakish half smile, was unmistakable. Tannis was female, and Alex had morphed into … flirting mode? My stomach did a little flip-flop and I felt like all the blood had rushed out of my head.

I spun around, stomped into the kitchen, and gathered Vinnie's food, a spare litter box, and litter, shoving it all into a large shopping bag. I then went into the hall and flung open the closet door to retrieve the cat carrier. The only time the carrier came out was when Vinnie was going to the vet, so I surreptitiously deposited it behind the now open door so he wouldn't freak out if he saw it.

"Hailey, are you alright? You seem a bit agitated."

"I'm fine," I proclaimed tersely as I moved into the bedroom and sat down on the side of my bed.

Sebastian was silent for a moment and then said, *"My dear, don't try to fool me. I can sense your disquiet. Your blood pressure had increased and your adrenaline rush is making me jittery."*

"Well, let's see. I have to sneak out of town because some whack job, oh wait, some supernatural whack job, may or may not want to kill me or something. Who wouldn't be upset?"

"But why the abrupt change? One minute you are imperturbable and the next you are ready to explode. Unless…"

"Unless what?"

"You were fine until Alexander placed his call to his … assistant."

"Oh, Tannis is his assistant?"

I tried to sound nonchalant, but must not have done a convincing job, because Sebastian howled with laughter. *"I knew it! You are jealous!"*

My cheeks flushed but I was determined to keep up the charade that I had no interest in what kind of assistance Tannis gave Alex. Unfortunately, all I could come up with was the not particularly clever, and most assuredly infantile, "I am not!" in response.

"Please forgive my presumptuousness," he chortled. *"But if you did happen to feel some rivalry for Alexander's affection, you have little reason to worry."*

"Well, judging from his end of the conversation, they seemed pretty chummy."

"True, they are well acquainted—known each other for years, in fact. But I am quite certain that his interest in Tannis is decidedly not libidinous."

"Why, is she married, or old and ugly?" Either would do.

"On the contrary, she is single and quite beautiful indeed; looks a bit like your Rachel, but taller and more… ethereal."

Great. Now I had a mental image of a hotter version of my way-hot best friend to further enrage the green-eyed monster that was already fighting to overwhelm me.

Through clenched teeth, I managed to force out a clipped, "Sebastian, this is so not helping. What part of that description would lead you to believe that Alex wouldn't be attracted to her?"

"Because Tannis is Alexander's sister."

"His sister," I echoed back. "His sister? Why didn't you mention that at the beginning? You just spent the last few minutes jerking me around, you bastard!"

Peals of laughter rang out in my head and it was a few moments before Sebastian's cackling subsided enough for him to speak.

"And you claimed you were not jealous. The enmity was practically oozing from your pores."

I lowered my voice so Alex would be less likely to hear. "Stop it, this isn't funny."

I was mortified that Sebastian had assessed my feelings so easily, angry that he found it amusing, and somewhat mystified that any of it would matter to me. After all, for years, I'd successfully buried any thoughts of a relationship, and I'd only known Alex for a short time. To top it all off, I could feel my eyes beginning to well with tears, and I'd be damned if I was going to let Sebastard make me cry.

As I tried to get control of myself, Sebastian's voice filled my head once more, but this time his tone was softer.

"It is obvious to me that you are attracted to Alexander and it is equally apparent that he is attracted to you. Why pretend that you were not concerned that you might have a rival?"

I didn't respond, partly because I was still irritated, but mostly because I wasn't certain I had completely contained the waterworks. Sebastian was, of course, unaffected by my silence and continued with his commentary.

"Life is short, my dear. You must not let what happened in your past prevent you from finding happiness."

I was pretty sure that the only reason he was pitching this was to fulfill his own erotic fantasies, but I was in no mood to discuss his possible motivations. I stood, picked up Vinnie—who had been sleeping on some freshly laundered towels that were stacked on my dresser—gave him a big hug, and jammed him into the carrier before he had a chance to shred the crap out of me.

~12~

Alex and Sebastian wanted to take no chances that whoever was asking questions at O'Reilly's had us under surveillance. So, the plan was for me to drop Vinnie off at Rachel and Harrison's, drive back home where Alex and I would sneak out and circle around to an out-of-the-way spot where he had hidden his rental car and our luggage. We even put Vinnie's carrier inside a large, canvas shopping bag so anyone watching wouldn't suspect we were leaving town.

As Harrison let me into their apartment, he stared at the bagged cat carrier and frowned, apparently confused by the odd presentation. Fast on my feet, I quickly came up with the story that Vinnie was calmer in the car if the carrier was covered, and Harrison seemed to buy the explanation.

Now inside, I pulled the transport cage from the sack, placed it on the floor next to the sectional sofa, and opened the door. Vinnie poked his head out, but wouldn't leave the horrible box he spent the entire, interminable ride objecting to with ear-piercing howls. *Stupid cat.*

"Thanks for taking care of the beast on such short notice; I really appreciate it."

Rachel reached down and scratched behind Vinnie's ears, still flattened in anger because of his unfair treatment. "Don't worry about Vinnie, he'll be fine."

I handed over the other bag containing the kitty accoutrements to Harrison, and said goodbye to Vinnie. He meowed in response, but I knew he was already plotting his revenge.

"I'll let you know how long I'll be gone as soon as I can," I said to Rachel, as she walked me out to my car.

"No rush. Have fun with the nieces."

"Excellent improvisation in response to the query about the bagged cat," Sebastian said approvingly as I started the car. *"Your ability to deceive is exemplary, my dear."*

I supposed the comment was meant as a compliment, but I found it disconcerting how easily I crafted the lie. I kept telling myself that this was all to make sure no one else was in danger, but felt terrible keeping my friends in the dark.

At home, I made certain that the timers my parents gave me for Christmas were set properly to turn lights and the TV on and off. When I'd opened the present, I remember thinking it was a pretty lame gift I'd never use. Maybe my parents knew that one day I'd have to flee my home and would need gadgets to make it appear I was still in residence. If I managed to make it out of this mess in one piece, I'd have to thank them more sincerely when next I saw them.

Once everything was in place, Alex and I slipped out the back door. His car was parked only a half-mile away, but because of the circuitous route he chose, it took us close to forty minutes before we hit the road.

He headed south, keeping mainly to lightly traveled roads where anyone following would be easier to notice. We left the city and drove in silence until I asked where we were going.

"There's an airstrip near Sonoita. I have arranged for someone to pick us up and fly us to New Hampshire."

I wasn't thrilled about having to take a small plane. The thought of flying on a big jet, which I had assumed would be our mode of travel, had made me nervous enough, but now I wished I had the foresight to pack some Dramamine. Well, Alex had already witnessed me clumsy, naked, and hysterical; nauseated would just add to the ever-growing list of unflattering predicaments in which he'd seen me.

"You don't happen to have a magical solution for airsickness, do you? I'm not the greatest flyer."

Alex glanced over at me, smiled, and patted my knee. "You're in luck; I'm quite adept at conjuring anti-emetic spells." He lowered his voice to add, "It is not unusual for the novice *Xyzok* to need it after some of the more graphic training videos."

I didn't know if I should be shocked or disgusted, nor if he was being completely serious. I guess fighting supernatural bad guys was not unlike standard police work in that, occasionally, something totally revolting happened. Still, I was happy that running a chinchilla milking operation was pretty much gore-free.

I glanced at Alex's stunning face, illuminated only by the glow of the dashboard lights, and pondered what kinds of nasty things he'd witnessed. Or perpetrated, for that matter. Those scars he had probably didn't come from innocuous events, but I wasn't sure I was ready to find out exactly how he got them, either.

We continued a while longer on paved roads until Alex pulled off onto the shoulder and studied the GPS that was built into the dashboard. He then reached into the back seat and grabbed a backpack, from which he produced a small, portable GPS receiver.

"I know we are close to where we have to leave the main road. Before we left, I marked the general area on the car's GPS, but I also programmed the specific coordinates into the handheld."

He powered it up and punched a few buttons before handing the GPS to me, explaining that it would beep when we reached the turn off. He pulled back onto the road, and about a mile or so ahead, the device let us know we needed to turn.

Alex slowed the car, and immediately to our right was what looked like a dirt driveway that hadn't been used in years. The outline of a cleared path was visible, but there were so many weeds and rocks it was unlikely anyone would randomly choose to drive over such a poorly maintained area.

"Are you sure this car can make it?" I questioned, wondering if a Ford Taurus had enough ground clearance to navigate the primitive thoroughfare.

"I have faith in American automotive engineering. Besides, it's a rental, so it's no big deal if it bottoms out," he added with a mischievous grin.

A few bumpy minutes later, we arrived at a clearing. Waiting there were two men in a Jeep Wrangler, its mud-caked and dented exterior suggested it was used frequently for some heavy-duty off-roading. Alex greeted the men warmly, first in Courso, then shifting to English when he introduced me.

"Hailey, this is Aiden and Cortez. They are co-workers of mine. Aiden will take us the rest of the way to the airstrip and Cortez will take the Taurus and return it to the rental agency."

I nodded and shook their hands. Both men were shorter than Alex, but still fairly tall. The similarity ended there, however. Aiden looked like Opie from Mayberry with boyish good looks, coppery red hair, pale complexion, and freckles, while Cortez seemed like he'd walked out of a *Telenovela*—darkly handsome with smoldering eyes and skin the color of an expensive, cream-laden coffee drink.

Aiden regarded at me as if he was staring into my soul. After a few moments, he turned to Alex and said,

"When you told me about Sebastian deconverging into another, I thought you were making it up. He always claimed it could be done, and I always thought he was full of shit. Now that I am near her, however, I can feel his signature. It's ... remarkable."

Sebastian snorted derisively in my head. *"Why should he be so surprised? Remarkable people do remarkable things."*

Alex wasn't in physical contact with me so he didn't hear Sebastian, but said, "Yes, it is remarkable, but keep this information to yourselves. This isn't something that needs to be common knowledge."

Aiden's face suddenly became somber. "You know you can trust us. We would give our lives for you or Sebastian, and if you ask, we will take this to our graves."

Alex nodded, placed his hand on Aiden's shoulder and murmured something in Courso. He motioned to Cortez and repeated the gesture and words to him. Both men then took a step backward, lowered their heads, and placed their right hand across to the left side of their upper chest. Alex gestured in kind before their posture relaxed and everyone was smiling again. I wasn't exactly sure what had just transpired, but the deference shown to Alex by both men reminded me of soldiers to their commanders or commoners to royalty. There was obviously more to it than just co-workers, and I made a mental note to ask Alex about it later.

We transferred our luggage to the Jeep and Alex tossed his keys to Cortez, who gave us a mock salute before climbing into the Taurus.

"Not much of a talker, is he?" I remarked as Mr. Mochaccino drove away.

"He's in a hurry; there's a *Three Stooges* marathon on tonight and he forgot to record it," Aiden replied. He opened the door of the Jeep and flipped up the passenger-side seat so I could get into the back. "Never get between Cortez and Moe, Larry, and Curly."

"Huh, all this time, I pictured the Coursodon as superior beings. But it's comforting to know that the inexplicable male fondness for the Stooges transcends dimensions."

Alex seemed perplexed. "What's not funny about them? We consider them to be comic geniuses and one of the few artistic highpoints of modern humanity."

I started to laugh, but from both Alex and Aiden's expressions, I quickly realized that what I initially thought was sarcasm was meant with complete candor. "Do you think the same thing about Jerry Lewis?"

"Of course not," Aiden huffed. "We're not French."

"If it is any consolation, my dear, I find slapstick comedy to be sophomoric and tedious. Please do not judge us all based on the atrocious predilections of these philistines."

"Hey guys, Sebastian says you have lousy taste in humor."

Alex scoffed. "We have lousy taste? Isn't that the pot calling the kettle black?"

"No shit," Aiden growled. "Sebastian thinks Pauly Shore is hysterical."

"Who's Pauly Shore?" I asked.

"My point exactly," Aiden replied.

"Oh, my dear, your ignorance wounds me to the core. And I had such high hopes for you."

I shrugged and raised my hands in surrender. "Apparently, you all have questionable preferences in humor. Remind me to never let any of you chose a comedy on movie night."

I folded myself into the backseat and we continued through the dark, cold desert for another hour. On the far side of a hill was a long stretch of pavement, at the end of which sat a Learjet. Basically, all aircraft looked pretty much the same to me and the only reason I knew it was a Learjet was that it had *Learjet* written on the side. Apart from the headlights of the Jeep, however, there was no additional illumination, the absence of which bumped my pre-flight anxiety up a few notches.

"How does it take off in the dark?" I whispered nervously as we got out of the Jeep.

"Like this," a feminine voice announced behind us. I turned around just as the owner of the voice snapped her fingers and the runway was suddenly outlined in small, bright, bluish lights.

"Angelica!" Alex exclaimed. "I had no idea you would be here tonight. How's my favorite pilot?"

She walked past me and gave Alex a hug, which he followed with a brief kiss on each of her cheeks.

"When I heard you needed a ride, I made sure I got the assignment," she purred while slowly tracing a finger along Alex's jaw.

Angelica's silky, blue-black hair was long and styled with loose waves that were meant to seem carefree and casual, but probably took an hour to perfect. The darkness of her tresses was in stark contrast to her ice-blue eyes, the color accentuated by the expertly applied, smoky-violet eyeliner that encircled them. Curvy in all the right places, even in the plain white blouse and utilitarian navy trousers that comprised her uniform, she oozed sensuality. That she was currently directing her *fuck me* vibe at Alex, made me immediately loathe her.

Alex smoothly removed Angelica's hand and turned her around to face me.

"Ang, this is Hailey."

I put out my hand—not that I really wanted her to shake it, but my mother always taught me to act civil even when I wasn't feeling it. Without any movement to accept my polite gesture, Angelica looked me over dismissively, then said to Alex, "We'd better get rolling, it's a long flight." Then, she sashayed toward the plane, swinging her ample hips to their fullest potential.

I stood there for a moment, my mouth agape over her shameless bad manners. And really, Angelica? When choosing her human name, she was either deluding herself or heavily into irony. My hatred towards her was growing by the second.

Alex followed, but stopped Devilica about twenty feet away with a tap on the shoulder. He began talking, but they were too far away for me to hear anything.

"It's too bad I don't have your heightened Courso aural senses," I whispered petulantly to Sebastian.

"Fortunately, I can tell exactly what is being said."

"But I thought you could only sense things as I do because you're using my body, and I can't make out one word."

"Yes, your human ears are quite deficient. I, however, can read lips."

"Really? Why would someone with preternatural hearing learn to lip read?"

"It is a skill that comes in handy when in a crowded room filled with many voices. It has saved me any number of times in my career. It is so useful, in fact, I taught Alexander how to do it as well."

I immediately turned my back on Alex and Angelica. "So, what were they saying?"

Sebastian laughed quietly. *"Well, she was turned away from us, so I could only catch Alexander's part. He did say, 'Hailey is very important to me, so behave yourself.'"*

Satisfaction washed over me. *All right, Alex!* My exhilaration was somewhat tempered when I considered that his estimation of my importance might be more related to harboring Sebastian than because of any feelings he might have for me. I turned back around just in time to see Bitchelica's bottom lip poke out in a pout before she continued her butt swing to the jet. Well, whatever Alex's motivation, at least I was content with the knowledge that now I wasn't the only one ticked off.

As I walked toward the steps extending from the open door of the plane, Sebastian spoke again. *"I think there is hope for you yet. You turned away on purpose so Alexander would not be able to read your lips, yes?"*

"Yeah, so what if I did?" I snapped impatiently.

"I meant it as a compliment. You did it almost instinctively, without thought. You possess an inner shrewdness that is commendable. You know, if not for the fact that you are human, you would make an excellent Xyzok."

"Right. I don't think I'm enough of a macho, badass for that."

"Well, forgoing any obvious retorts concerning the quality of your derrière, one does not need to be particularly physically rugged to be effective in the job. I believe that you possess the intelligence and mental fortitude required."

I didn't agree with Sebastian's assessment. "Sure, I'm smart enough, but mental toughness? No way."

"I think you underestimate yourself. I wager that before our adventure is completed, your grit will be revealed."

Not knowing what else to say, I simply walked past Alex—who was still standing in the spot where he and that woman had their discussion—and started up the stairs to the plane. I don't know why I was miffed at him, he had chastised her on my behalf, but now, I was being rude. Stopping my ascent at the middle stair, I turned around and said, "Sorry, I thought we were in a hurry," and then waited for him to catch up. *Take that, Mom. And you thought I wasn't paying attention.*

While smaller than a commercial airplane, the Learjet was way better. There were eight large, leather-upholstered seats, and the flight attendant—Paul—a short slip of a fellow with a shaved head and a goatee, explained that they were fully reclinable. This was good news; on the few occasions I had flown, I couldn't fall asleep sitting up. When I did manage to nod off, my head flopped oddly from side to side, giving me neck cramps for days afterward.

Paul described the extensive food and beverage choices, which all sounded much more appealing than the overpriced snack boxes offered on my last airplane ride. I asked for a cup of black tea and a glass of ice to make iced tea and was pleasantly surprised when he informed me that, per Alex's instructions, a pitcher of my beverage of choice, freshly brewed, was already prepared. *That's service.*

We chose two adjacent seats, and while Paul went to get our drinks, I realized that, particularly when this close to the Mexican border, our travel could be easily misconstrued by any number of law enforcement agencies.

"Aren't you concerned that Homeland Security or the DEA will notice a small plane taking off from an isolated airstrip?"

"That's where the ability to use magic comes in handy. The runway and plane are undetectable to anyone other than us."

That was a neat trick. "Between keeping the existence of another dimension secret and cleaning up after Courso criminals, that's probably a plus in a whole bunch of situations."

Before Alex could respond, Paul delivered our drinks and made certain we were buckled in before moving to the back of the plane for takeoff. Once the attendant was safely out of earshot, Alex leaned toward me and said, "Incidentally, I apologize for Angelica's discourteous behavior. I'm not really sure why she had such an intense reaction to you."

I looked at him with both amusement and incredulity. *No idea?* "You didn't date her by any chance, did you?"

"Well, no one really dates Angelica." When I raised a questioning eyebrow, he added, "We had a few... casual encounters, but the last was at least five years ago. But that doesn't explain her being discourteous."

I shook my head. *Men.* Apparently, cluelessness concerning the female psyche spanned dimensions.

"You didn't have to have a relationship with her," I explained, air-quoting *relationship*. "Just because you only hooked up a few times doesn't mean she doesn't feel some possessiveness over you. She probably thought you were rubbing me in her face." The mental picture that statement conjured made me want to gag.

Alex looked completely shocked. "Why would she feel that way? I don't think we ever even went out on an actual date. And it's not like she ever did anything to indicate that she wanted or expected more."

"Regardless, she obviously feels her over-developed, tawdry sex-goddess self-esteem is being threatened."

Sebastian chose that moment to add his two cents to the conversation. *"Really, my dear, you are making it seem as if you are castigating Alexander and defending Angelica."*

"Believe me, I'm not defending her." *I might slap her, though.* "I'm just trying to point out why she might be acting like a total bitch."

In response, Alex and Sebastian simultaneously muttered, "Women," which made me laugh.

She might have been an envious, ill-mannered harlot, but she definitely knew how to fly. The liftoff was smooth and I settled in for the long flight east. Alex held my hand and eventually began a tactical dialogue with Sebastian. The electrical buzz created by their connection coupled with the constant droning of the plane's engines made me very sleepy, so I flattened my seat and promptly was out like a light.

I woke up a couple hours later to find Alex fully reclined and dozing, still grasping my hand. His head was angled toward me and I took the opportunity to survey his striking features. Damn, he was fine. His shoulder-length hair, naturally the beautiful, light golden tone women paid their hairdressers tons of money to achieve, was usually pushed back away from his face. A piece in the front had fallen forward while he slept, and I had to stop myself from brushing the stray locks off his forehead to see if it felt as good as it looked.

As if he had somehow read my increasingly lustful thoughts, Alex's eyes opened. He smiled when our gazes met, and I felt my face begin to heat. I thought to myself, *really Hailey, aren't you a little old to still blush?* Which, of course, made me blush even more. Attempting to cover my self-consciousness, I restored my seat to an upright position and looked around as if I was trying to find Paul. I'm pretty sure that my act didn't fool Alex one bit, but he didn't comment, just squeezed my hand, and closed his eyes once more.

Hours later, our pilot's silky voice flowed out from the cockpit via the public-address system to let us know that we were ready to descend. It was daybreak in New Hampshire when we finally landed at a small, private airfield; snow blanketed everything except where the runway was cleared. A large, dark sedan sat idling near where the plane had stopped, the billowing, thick plumes of condensation from the vehicle's exhaust indicated it was mighty cold out there.

As we exited the jet, Go-to-hellica opened the cockpit door and motioned to Alex. I waited on the top stair while they spoke, shivering as the first bite of frigid air cut through my fleece jacket. Just as I was deciding whether to make a break for the warmth of the awaiting car or step back into the plane, Alex placed a hand on the small of my back and guided me down the stairs.

I glanced back to see her glaring at me, a triumphant smile curling across her lips. *What the hell?* Had she used the thirty seconds she had Alex's attention to schedule a hook up for later? I really hoped not, because if I saw her again anytime soon, I might have to put that ho in her place.

~13~

The safe house sat on the shore of a lake. There was a small town nearby, and while the density of homes in the area was high, it was located on a few acres of land in a less populated stretch. The outside was unassuming, a well-kept but plain, two-story, wooden structure with an inviting, wrap-around porch. The interior was similarly modest with simple, but tasteful, furnishings throughout. The first floor had a living room, dining area, kitchen, and two bedrooms connected by a full bathroom; upstairs there were five more small bedrooms and an additional bath.

Jonathan, our driver, deposited our bags inside and departed, having only uttered a heavily accented "hello" and "we're here" during the entire journey. He seemed friendly, though, and Alex explained that he was new and hadn't spent much time outside of Courso, and was probably not yet comfortable with human languages.

Alex closed the door behind the driver, entered a series of numbers into a keypad affixed to the wall near the front door and then turned to me and said, "You are now as safe as is possible in either dimension."

"Okay, I'll take your word for it, but aside from the burglar alarm you just activated, it seems just like any other house to me."

With a knowing grin, Alex directed me to what appeared to be a storage closet tucked under the stairs. He opened the door, yanked a string hanging from a ceiling fixture to turn on the light, and pulled me inside. The interior was exactly what one might expect—cramped, with coats hanging from a rod, with a few small boxes of stuff on a shelf above. I looked around the small space, and then arched an eyebrow.

"No offense, but I'm pretty sure the first place someone would look is in here."

"My dear, you really need to start thinking outside the box. Or the closet, as it were," Sebastian scolded.

Alex pushed aside the coats, ducked down, and moved into the angled space created by the rise of the staircase. Above his head, he touched a section of the wooded slats that comprised the ceiling and a small piece flipped down, exposing a panel with buttons and a flat, glassy surface. He laid his hand on the glass, which activated a beam of light that moved underneath his palm. Then he punched in a five-number sequence, and the floor at the farthest end of the space soundlessly slid open.

I peered, wide-eyed, into the hole in the floor. There was a spiral staircase, illuminated only by tiny lights along the edges of the treads, leading down.

"After you," Alex invited and I cautiously stepped onto what looked surprisingly like one of those lighted, spiral Christmas trees people use to decorate outdoors, but with the larger swirl on the top instead of at the base. I descended a few feet, then Alex followed and touched another pad that closed the closet floor over us. When what was now our ceiling was completely shut, lights came on, allowing an easy descent.

At the bottom was a small, concrete-walled chamber with an imposing metal door. Once again, Alex flattened his palm against a scanning device on the wall, this time speaking a short phrase rather than punching in a code, and the door swung open to reveal a large room, bustling with people and activity.

It was as if there was an entire office building under the house. Directly in front of us was an armed guy in a gray uniform who saluted Alex and nodded at me as we passed. There was a bank of cubicles on one side of the room, each manned and outfitted with a computer and other unidentifiable electronic gizmos. Glass-walled offices lined the opposite side, and in the center, was a lounge area, with people relaxing or socializing.

"Shit."

"I knew you would be impressed. Overwhelming, is it not?"

I was whatever was beyond overwhelmed—megawhelmed?

"What the hell is all this?"

Alex laughed. "I told you this place was safe. The house itself is like a mini fortress: ballistic glass on all windows, reinforced steel doors masquerading as wooden ones, and sophisticated security systems. Plus, there are screening methods in use that mask magical activity. If someone with bad intent managed to slip past all that, there's this hidden escape route. Down here, you have at least forty highly trained *Xyzok* that provide additional monitoring of the area. Beyond these offices are living spaces that crisscross with a number of tunnels that extend under the lake that provide a variety of ways for entrance or egress."

I was having some trouble taking it all in. "This must be like the secret, undisclosed location Dick Cheney used when he was Vice President."

"Oh, that pales in comparison. This is much more secure. Only a very few of the most select and trusted *Xyzok* even know this place exists."

"And now, me," I noted with growing unease.

"Do you know where we are?" Alex inquired.

Now that I thought about it, all I knew was that we were in New Hampshire. That could be a ruse as well, except I remembered seeing a lot of New Hampshire license plates on other vehicles while we were driving here.

"Ah, no, actually, we could be almost anywhere," I admitted.

"Exactly. And if you had to recall how you got here from the jet, could you?"

I tried to conjure up details of the ride, but for the life of me, couldn't recollect a single landmark or geographic feature that could help pinpoint our location.

"Did you do something to screw with my memory?" I grumbled.

"Not specifically, your inability to retrace your journey is just one of the safeguards."

"So, how come *you* remember where this place is? And what about Jonathan, you trust him with this information?"

"I have the highest security clearance, so I am exempt from the magical obfuscation. All those with lower-level clearance you see here today have agreed to have their memories altered when their deployment is over. They won't be able to reveal anything either by accident or coercion. As for Jonathan, he knows only that he drove us to a house. He has no idea what lies beneath, nor does anyone else that lives around here. All these workers and trainees come and go via the tunnels."

Why any of that should surprise me, given all that had happened of late, was a mystery, but I was still pretty blown away. Before I could fully process the complexity of the underground complex, Alex leaned in close, whispering directly into my ear. "By the way, almost everyone here will be able to sense Sebastian when they are close to you. Because we believe it is best to limit the number of people who are aware of the deconvergence, we had to devise a plausible explanation for his signature within you."

I was sure whatever they had come up with, I wasn't going to like. "Okay, out with it."

Alex took a deep breath. "You are pregnant and Sebastian is the father."

"That would explain his signature in me?"

He seemed relieved that I wasn't angry, so he continued with much more enthusiasm.

"Well, generally a developing fetus would emit a detectable pattern, albeit much weaker, of the Courso parent or parents. Even though Sebastian's aura in you is much stronger than what would be usual during pregnancy, people should chalk that up to Sebastian's prodigious power."

I wasn't completely comfortable with people thinking I was carrying Sebastian's child, but I couldn't put my finger on why it bothered me. Maybe I just didn't want to be seen as someone who got knocked up by a notorious womanizer. Maybe I was unsettled by the fact that there was no need for Courso paternity tests because everyone could essentially sniff out who's your daddy. Regardless of the reason, if the subterfuge made things easier for Alex, I could manage to deal with it.

"At least my mother will be thrilled if she hears about the virginal conception. She's always wanted me to embrace religion."

While I tried to decide how to play the role of expectant paramour, Alex mentioned that he needed to confer with someone regarding any new information about Otto. I waited on one of the leather couches in the room's center and concentrated on appearing nonchalant despite being anything but.

Soon, I was distracted from my efforts at character development when a woman with short, spiked purple hair and a septum piercing, slammed a stack of papers on the coffee table and flopped down next to me on the sofa. She cradled her head in her hands and let out an exasperated sigh before barking out something in Courso.

I had no clue why she was so upset, but not wanting to appear unfeeling, I said, "Unfortunately, I only speak English." She lifted her head and stared blankly. Concerned that my response may have seemed rude, I quickly added, "But, I can curse in about eight different languages."

"Oh, sorry. You have a strong signature, so I figured you were Courso. Anyway, I said this assignment is going to drive me insane!"

I tried to convey my understanding of her dilemma—after all, who hasn't been given some annoying task at work—with a shrug and a knowing nod. She took my response as an invitation to continue her complaints, however.

"I've only got one test left before I am fully certified in Decryption and Code Breaking, but I've been at this for days and I can't seem to get a toehold. I told them when I was accepted that I would suck at this, but would they listen? I wanted to specialize in Incursions, but instead they stick me in DCB."

To be polite, and because I really didn't know what else to say, I glanced over at her work, which was now strewn haphazardly before me. She pushed the papers around until she yanked out a page filled with only numbers. "I'm supposed to decipher this. I've tried everything and nothing has worked." She was almost shouting.

"So, what's all the rest of this?" I asked, flipping through the first couple of pages on top of the mess. It was all written in what I assumed was Courso, because there wasn't a single letter that I recognized. The unusual script was beautiful with both graceful swirls and almost geometric shapes—kind of like Greek meets Arabic.

"That's the supplemental information. Stuff found with, or related to, the hypothetical person that encoded the message. It's supposed to help me figure out what the hell this says."

She ran a hand through her spiky locks and grimaced. "I can sort of understand the benefit of knowing some of this crap, like when and where he was born and his political affiliations. But it is beyond me how knowing his alcoholic beverage of choice or his favorite song will be of any use."

This last bit made me take more notice. "His favorite song was included in the information you were given?"

"Yeah. And his favorite color is magenta, for all that's worth," she huffed.

"I could be completely off base here, but have you considered a VIC cipher?"

She looked at me like I had two heads.

"The VIC cipher," I explained, "is an old, Cold War-era field cipher that no one could break until some Russian spy defected and explained how it worked. It's not as secure as modern, computer driven codes, but it did the trick in the nineteen-fifties. It's complicated, but I remember that it used a few different steps, each of which required a different key. I'm pretty sure that the keys included the lyrics of a song, a date, and another random number."

Suddenly intrigued, she shifted her gaze back to the papers. "It never occurred to me to investigate human codes, although I should have, since the numbers aren't in Courso." She stood and quickly gathered the pile. "Wow, thanks for the info, maybe I'll finish this yet," she called out over her shoulder as she hurried away.

"Happy to help," I uttered to her retreating form.

"How do you know about VIC?"

I didn't realize that Alex had returned and I jumped a little when I heard his voice behind me.

When my heart stopped thumping wildly, I admonished him with, "Jeez, don't sneak up on a pregnant woman like that!"

"Sorry, little momma, but I was surprised that you would know so much about arcane encryption techniques.

Is that something everybody with a degree in physiology knows or have you been hiding your secret ties to the CIA from me?"

I briefly contemplated making up an interesting explanation, but settled for the truth instead.

"When I was an undergrad, I dated a guy that was obsessed with cryptography. He would send me encrypted, romantic notes and I would have to figure out what they said. They started out simple—you know, one letter substituted for another—then got progressively more difficult. I know it sounds really geeky, but they were like puzzles, and I was pretty adept at breaking them. The one he gave me that used VIC took me about a month to crack, and he further complicated it by making the first sentence complete gibberish, even when correctly decoded, to throw me off. I think I broke up with him after that."

"You are correct, my dear. That is extraordinarily geeky," Sebastian quipped.

I knew he couldn't see me roll my eyes, but I was pretty sure he'd be able to sense my exasperation, so I did it anyway.

Alex laughed. "I take it Sebastian was giving you grief over your former boyfriend's unusual seduction methods?"

"I knew I should have concocted a story that made me look better," I muttered under my breath.

"I'm not sure which is more impressive, your skill as a code cracker or your apparent ability to swear in a multitude of languages," Alex teased.

I hadn't realized that he had been standing there that long. "Thanks so much," I responded sarcastically. "I'm truly gifted."

"I am still trying to determine which is more troublesome, that you did not end your relationship despite this fellow's seriously inadequate romantic acumen, or that you did so because he used an added dimension of trickery to try to thwart you."

I'd really had enough. "Hey Sebastard," I sputtered. "Yumago! Do prdele! Haista paska! Jebiesz jeze! Foda-se!"

Obviously puzzled because he was not privy to the voice in my head, Alex raised one eyebrow before saying "What was all that?"

I stood and huffed out, "Korean, Czech, Finnish, Polish, and Portuguese!"

~14~

Alex didn't stop snickering at my Sebastian-directed tirade until well after we left the hidden command post and returned to the quiet of the house above. I realized that my outburst was out of proportion given the moderate amount of snark in Sebastian's assessment of my prior dalliances, but there was no way in hell I was going to apologize.

Unfortunately, my over-developed sense of right and wrong made me feel bad about that. Thus, I decided to check out the kitchen and see if there were sufficient quantities of either chocolate or tequila with which to assuage my guilt.

Whoever stocked the place made sure no one would ever go hungry. Baskets on the counters were filled with fruit and loaves of bread and a quick glance into the pantry revealed anything anyone could ever want or desire in the way of dry goods.

The fridge looked like the display case at a fancy delicatessen—there must have been eight kinds of cheese. It was also packed with sliced meats, salads, homemade soups, a giant veggie tray, various flavors and types of yogurt, and a plate of pastries that looked too perfect to eat. The freezer was filled with plastic containers labeled with delicious sounding things like eggplant parmesan, coq au vin, and lamb vindaloo and enough frozen desserts to make Baskin-Robbins jealous. There was so much, in fact, it made it difficult to decide what to eat.

I made it easy on myself and opted for a chocolate-covered éclair. I didn't even bother with a plate—I just ate it while standing with the refrigerator door still open.

As I was licking the last of the creamy custard filling from my fingers, Alex came in and set a bottle of Glen Fiddich and a bottle of Patron on the center island. Someone thought of everything, apparently.

"If those are éclairs in there, you better save me some, or I'm not sharing the alcohol."

"Deal. But the Rocket Pops are mine."

"What's a Rocket Pop?"

I was astounded. "Over one hundred years old, and you never heard of Rocket Pops? You have been missing a wondrous piece of Americana, my friend."

I opened the freezer, grabbed two popsicles, and handed one to Alex. I unwrapped mine to reveal the missile-shaped treat with its red layer on top, followed by a white mid-section, and ending with a layer of blue.

"The Rocket Pop," I began, gesturing at it like I was Vanna White showing what you've won, "is the quintessential Independence Day dessert that skillfully juxtaposes three delicious flavors in one yummy confection."

Alex did not seem convinced, but peeled away the paper on his and took a bite off the top. He rolled it around his mouth, swallowed, and then looked thoughtfully at what remained.

"Not bad. The top is cherry flavored, what do the other parts taste like?"

"The middle is kind of citrusy and the bottom…"

In truth, I had no idea what the bottom flavor was supposed to be. Alex looked at me expectantly. "The bottom tastes blue," I proclaimed.

He still looked skeptical, but took a tentative nibble from the bottom. "You're right. It definitely tastes blue," he said. "But I'm not sure I share your enthusiasm. I freely concede the Rocket Pops to you."

"Suit yourself, but don't come begging when you realize you've made an epoch gastronomic mistake."

"I seriously doubt anyone with even a modicum of culinary refinement would grieve if deprived of these things," Sebastian snorted dismissively.

I pondered that for a moment as I finished the last of my popsicle. "Maybe it's an acquired taste, but believe me, on a sweltering day, there's nothing better."

"I suppose that could explain my somewhat underwhelming reaction. It is, after all, below freezing outside at the moment. Maybe if you dipped it in the scotch?"

Despite having eaten dessert first, Alex and I were still hungry. We heated up some lobster bisque and made smoked turkey sandwiches. Everything was delicious, and I used a leftover bit of sandwich crust to mop up the very last of the soup in my bowl.

"Whoever provided the food is my hero," I stated contentedly.

"The support staff downstairs does it. If there's anything that you want that isn't here already, let me know. They will obtain it and bring it up."

Given the wide variety of provisions currently on hand, I couldn't imagine needing anything else.

"There's more than enough food here. Didn't they realize it was just the two of us?"

"Well, it's a bit more complicated than that, actually. To be on the safe side, I thought it would be best if we kept a low profile and not venture into town. Because we can't run out to the grocery store ourselves if we need something, they went a little overboard because the dietitians were concerned that you might have cravings."

I could tell from his expression that Alex was bracing for me to get mad, and hoping that I wouldn't. I didn't like that he thought I might not be able to go with the flow, or the lack thereof given my pseudo condition.

"Look, I get why people have to think I'm pregnant. And while I admit that, at first, I was none too happy about it, if I'd known carrying Sebastian junior would get me access to all this fine eating, I would have been on board from the get-go. So, stop worrying."

"I was a bit concerned that the pregnancy ruse was asking too much. We have disrupted your life and you have done everything we have asked, regardless of the potential danger. You haven't had much choice in all this, and I want you to know how grateful I am that it was you who received Sebastian's Kindle."

"Indeed, my dear. You are a credit to your species."

This sudden wave of gratitude took me aback. Alex looked so sincere that I fought my initial urge to temper their praise with my usual glib responses. I really needed to work on my non-facetious communication skills.

Unfortunately, in the absence of smart-ass, my response was an ineloquent, "Wow, guys. Uh … thanks."

The ensuing silence was as uncomfortable as my inability to receive compliments with grace and self-assurance. Fortunately, the ringing of Alex's phone dispelled the awkwardness, and he went into the living room to take the call. When he'd finished, enough time had elapsed that other priorities required attention and the conversation was, thankfully, not picked up where we left off.

To not waste energy heating the upstairs, we decided to use only the two downstairs bedrooms. Alex put my bag in the one that faced the lake, but the frosty window made it difficult to see anything. I used a blow dryer in the cabinet under the bathroom sink to warm the glass enough to take in the view.

The lake was probably beautiful when not frozen solid—but now the smooth, glassy surface was stark and uninviting, and the absence of any soothing sounds of gentle waves lapping against the nearby shore made the wide expanse of thick ice even more austere. The leafless, snow-dusted trees surrounding the lake were spectacular, however, particularly when the sun glistened off them. I hadn't spent any time in this type of climate, and its novelty made it immediately appealing. Still, I was thrilled I didn't have to spend an entire winter here.

The next few days were filled with a lot of doing nothing particularly productive. We were still waiting for some credible information about the location of Sebastian's body and for me at least, it was way too cold to go outside. Alex was often occupied with following up leads, so I amused myself with my newly created, fake Facebook page playing online games. I could have used the time pursuing more intellectually stimulating endeavors, but most of the books I found in the house were either saccharine romances filled with throbbing members and heaving breasts, or dense historical novels filled with parliament members and dictators beating their chests. Even though, at Alex's request, I brought the Kindle along, given the events of the last few weeks, there was no way I was firing up that Pandora's Box.

There was lots of time to eat, and the wide array of goodies coupled with my reluctance to venture outside was making me sluggish. When I mentioned this to Alex, he introduced me to the underground workout facility, which conveniently provided weight-training and elliptical machines, along with a running track and a lap pool. There was even a place to get a massage. It was like a weird, militarized spa.

By the end of the fifth day, however, the novelty was wearing thin. I enjoyed spending time with Alex, and even the verbal sparring with Sebastian, but I had been doing that at home. I was tired of being cooped up in unfamiliar surroundings and I missed my cat. I was also losing patience with people's pitying looks when they encountered the poor human, incubating her presumed dead, man-ho lover's child. One afternoon, while in the sauna with one such sympathetic soul, I amused myself by confiding in her that I was originally unsure of who was the father, but before Sebastian's signature developed, I had the baby's paternity narrowed down between him and the offensive line of the Arizona Cardinals. Sure, it was sophomoric, but it made Sebastian cackle for the rest of the day.

The lack of progress must have bothered Alex as well—he seemed much more fidgety than normal. We had planned to watch yet another pay-per-view movie, but after finishing dinner, we decided neither of us was in the mood. Instead, we sat on the couch in front of the big stone fireplace and just talked.

The conversation was casual, and when he started reminiscing about his earlier days as Sebastian's apprentice, I realized that I had absolutely no idea what Sebastian looked like. I asked, but instead of a verbal description, Alex extended his hand, palm up, and soon a cloudy image appeared in the center. In another second or so, a three-dimensional image of a man, handsome and sporting a rather amused smirk, came into focus, floating a half-inch or so above Alex's hand.

"This is Sebastian," Alex said as the figure rotated slowly so I could see it from different angles.

Based solely on his voice, I had always pictured him as impeccably groomed with not a hair out of place. Surprisingly, he seemed more rugged than I expected, as if he had spent a lot of time climbing mountains or sailing the oceans.

Sebastian looked like he was fortyish, with straight, shoulder-length dark hair pulled back in a low ponytail, with a touch of grey at the temples. His features were masculine, with an aquiline nose, chiseled jaw, and cleft chin.

It was difficult to judge his height, but he was heavily muscled—not like Alex's sinewy, swimmer's body—but bulkier, like a football player. Even in holographic form, he looked confident and powerful. I could see why women would find his attractive, bad-boy appearance appealing.

"Pretty studly," I acknowledged.

"Thank you, I am indeed. Although I fear Alex's rendition pales in comparison to the real thing."

I relayed Sebastian's self-aggrandizing retort, Alex snickered and closed his hand, causing the image to fade away. "It is a challenge duplicating that which makes you so very ... you."

"That's a pretty cool trick," I said, gesturing at Alex's now Sebastianless hand. Can everyone conjure up something like that?"

Alex nodded. "It does eliminate the need to carry photographs in one's wallet."

I went over to the fireplace and as I tossed a new log onto the now dwindling flames, some of the glowing embers flew up, burning my exposed forearm.

"God fucking damn it, that hurts!" I shouted, waving my arm frantically.

I started to move toward the kitchen to run cold water over the painful, red blotch that had already begun to blister, but Alex stopped me.

Calmly placing his fingers just over the burned area, a cool sensation wafted down from his hand. Within a few seconds, the pain subsided. I examined my arm and was surprised that not only did it no longer hurt, but the blisters were gone, too. Only some residual redness remained.

Alex surveyed his work. "That was a nasty burn. You should be more careful next time. It might stay red for a day or so, but other than that, you shouldn't have any problems."

"And I thought the holographic Sebastian was amazing," I said, poking tentatively at the now healed flesh. "As long as you're fixing stuff, can you make my thighs thinner?"

Alex must not have realized I was joking.

"Healing is an entirely different matter than changing the way one looks," he explained. "If I maintained physical contact, I could alter your appearance, but once the connection ended, so would the modifications. I could change myself for a longer period, but it would take a lot of magic and it would not be permanent."

I remembered him telling me something about this before, when he was describing how the Coursodon might have been responsible for werewolf folklore because some had the ability to make themselves look like animals.

"I was just kidding about the magical liposuction, but just for fun, I've always wondered what I would look like as a blonde."

He frowned slightly, and I figured I had crossed some inter-dimensional line of propriety. I was about to apologize, when he guided me into the bathroom. Alex positioned me in front of the mirror over the sink, and stood behind me with his hands resting on my shoulders. He closed his eyes for a moment and I felt magic tingling from his fingertips into my shoulders. Then, my hair was the same color as his—golden, with lighter highlights.

It was cool, but also disappointing. I definitely wasn't meant to be fair-haired; the lighter tone washed me out and my hair reminded me off a dandelion, gone to seed.

"Huh. Not quite the transformation I was hoping for."

He removed his hands and my hair returned to its normal color.

"Why would you want to look different?" he asked, a perplexed look spreading across his face, reflected in the mirror.

"Oh, I don't know. I've always wanted to look less ordinary."

He frowned again, but said nothing. Replacing his hands on my shoulders, I felt the electric buzz once again. This time, however, he didn't close his eyes, but using the mirror, stared into mine. I found myself staring back, fixated only on his hypnotic gaze, until he said, "Look" and inclined his head toward the mirror.

No longer focused on Alex's reflection, I peered at my own, but a stranger greeted me. I couldn't quite put my finger on what was different, but every part of my face looked … better. My curls were shiny and luxurious and looked like I'd just spent hundreds of dollars at a salon. My skin glowed from within. Even my run-of-the-mill eyes seemed a deeper and more striking brown.

"Wow. I don't know what you just did, but I look phenomenal."

Without moving his hands, Alex leaned down and whispered, "All I did was let you see yourself the way I see you."

Flustered, I dropped my head so I didn't have to look at him.

"Don't you know how beautiful you are?"

"Oh sure, if boring eyes and hair and unremarkable features are considered attractive," I mumbled.

Alex turned me around so that we faced one another, or would have if I didn't still have my chin jammed into my sternum. He gently lifted my head until I couldn't avoid his now heated and intense gaze—his voice alone was like a caress.

"Unremarkable? Hailey, you are stunning. Your eyes are not boring, they are dark and mysterious, and I want to find out all the secrets locked behind them every time I look at you." He smiled and brushed a stray curl off my forehead. "And your hair is a gorgeous shade of chestnut; when you stand in the sun, it is alight with strands of copper and gold."

Before I could concoct another smart-ass comment to counter my feelings of unease, Alex softly pressed his lips to mine. Then he twined his hands in my hair and slowly trailed kisses from my forehead down to my neck and back up before he found my mouth once more.

This time, it was more fervent and my lips parted as his tongue skillfully stroked them. The heat that moments ago had flooded my face had now moved much lower, and definitely not from being embarrassed. Although if we continued with what we were currently doing, *bare-assed* wouldn't be far away.

I stood on my toes, but the difference in our heights made kissing standing up awkward. He quickly solved this logistical dilemma by lifting me onto the counter, his mouth never leaving mine. Now comfortably seated, I wrapped my legs around his waist and nestled my hands between the collar of his flannel shirt and the back of his neck.

Alex must have liked this new arrangement, if the low groan and grinding of his hips was any indication. The rhythmic pressure of his now obvious arousal moving against me was going to quickly send me over the edge. And I really, really wanted to go over—maybe more than once if I was lucky.

I vaguely considered getting a hold of myself—although Alex had pretty much taken care of that now that his hand had found its way under my shirt and was currently teasing my right nipple.

Then, I remembered we weren't really alone. As much as I wanted Alex, as much as I longed to have him inside me, I was, unfortunately, full up already.

As if he had the same thought, Alex pulled back slightly, sighed deeply, and leaned his forehead against mine.

"God, I can't believe I'm going to say this," he said, his voice ragged. "Please don't be mad, and this in no way has anything to do with how I feel about you or how much I want to continue this, but I don't think I can while you and Sebastian are ..."

I placed a finger to his lips to silence him and gazed into those impossibly blue eyes.

With both frustration and acceptance, I admitted, "I can't do it either, damn it," then scooted back on the counter to increase the distance between us. "But as soon as he is back where he belongs, you're mine, Blondie."

I was rewarded with one of his mind-bogglingly breathtaking smiles.

"I'll hold you to that," he said as he tenderly kissed the top of my head. "But for now, if you don't mind, I'd like to take a very long and very cold shower. You can take one after I'm done."

"Are you crazy? I haven't warmed up since we got here. Besides, I know a better way of dispelling sexual tension that doesn't include freezing myself."

I left the bathroom and retreated to my room counting, "One hundred, ninety-three ..."

***

After fifteen minutes, I was only at sixty-something. Counting backwards by sevens was not easy for me under normal conditions, but I kept getting distracted thinking about what had just almost happened and had to start over about eight or nine times. I finally gave up, changed into shorts and a long-sleeved, thermal-weave shirt, and got into bed.

When Alex finally emerged from his shower and peered at me from just outside the open door of my bedroom, he was wearing almost the same outfit as mine, except his shirt didn't have little pink bunnies.

"You know, Alex, just because we can't euphemistically sleep together doesn't mean we can't actually sleep together."

I hadn't planned on saying that, maybe Sebastian was influencing me to invite Alex into my bed to assuage his own sexual frustrations. Whatever the motivation, I just wanted to be held.

"I can do that."

He climbed under the covers and reached across to turn off the lamp on the nightstand. I rolled on my side, and he enveloped me with his long, warm arms, molding his body to mine. It felt nice to be spooned. It would have been better to be forked, but at this point, I would take whatever I could get.

We lay there silently, and as I was almost asleep, he nuzzled my neck and murmured softly, "Good night, my sweet."

~15~

The next morning when I woke up, Alex was on his back and I was snuggled against him, my head on his chest. I watched him sleep for a few minutes and took in every gorgeous feature of his relaxed face. When he opened his eyes and saw me looking at him, he smiled and draped his arm over my waist.

"Morning," he said sleepily, and leaned over to kiss me. "I must admit, I would have preferred making love to you all night long, but waking up with you is not bad."

We were already pressed together, and when he kissed me again, I had to force myself not to roll on top of him.

"This is harder than I thought," I muttered through clenched teeth.

Alex looked at me with a hooded gaze and a devilish grin.

"Thank you."

I was confused at first. Then I caught his meaning, which had nothing to do with the difficulty of restraining our passions until we were Sebastian-free. Or, maybe it did. I laughed but gave him a playful punch in the ribs.

"You know what I meant, and talking about what you meant isn't helping." In fact, now that was all I could think about.

To avoid temptation, I begrudgingly got out of bed. I took a shower, not a cold one, but going through my regular morning routine did manage to ratchet down my lust to a tolerable level.

Alex was eating a bowl of cereal when I finally made my way into the kitchen, from which wafted the enticing scents of freshly made coffee mixed with something sweet. I poured myself a cup, added just enough cream and sugar to mollify Sebastian without repulsing myself, and breathed in the rich, fragrant aroma before taking my first sip.

Alex looked up at me from his seat at the table. "I made some cranberry-orange muffins. They will be out of the oven in minute or two."

So that was the source of the sugary smell. *Could it get much better than this?* I wondered.

"You know, there's nothing sexier than a man who can bake."

"If I had known that, I would have been wooing you with my skills as a pastry chef from the beginning."

His use of the word "wooing" made me smile. Most of the time, it was easy to forget he was old enough to be my great-great grandfather. After all, he barely looked thirty—but every so often, he used some outdated term or phrase that made me remember not just his age, but that he wasn't of this world.

Human or not, the guy made a mean muffin. The first bite into the warm, moist goodie made me swoon.

"Oh my god, this is fantastic!" I moaned, greedily consuming the rest of the little piece of perfection.

I ate two in rapid succession before realizing that Alex was gazing at me, wide-eyed and grinning from ear to ear.

I planned to say, "Sorry, I didn't mean to go crazy, but they are delicious" but I was still chewing, so I only got out what sounded like, "swurry, I dint men to gwo cwatzy" before I covered my mouth with my napkin and started laughing.

Alex reached across the table and laced his fingers in mine. "I hope I get the same reaction when we finally make love," he said with a wink.

Hearing that made my groin clench, and even though my heavy sweater prevented me from being certain, I was pretty sure my nipples were erect, and I wasn't cold.

"If you make love the way you bake, it's a sure thing," I replied as I took a swig of coffee and grabbed another muffin. "But you've got to stop saying stuff like that, or Sebastian or no Sebastian, I won't be able to control myself."

"I just want to be sure you don't lose interest," he said with a smile that promised his interest was far from waning. His voice was rich and seductive, and it was likely that whatever he said, unless it concerned oozing pustules or parasitic worms, was going to arouse me. I'd just have to learn to deal.

After breakfast, Alex went down to the compound while I hung out in the house. It was still cold, but clear, so I bundled up in every bit of clothing I had and sat in the sun on the back porch for a while. It was weird, I was kind of hot and cold at the same time, but I enjoyed getting outside. Being this far north, winter days provided fewer hours of daylight than I was accustomed to back home, and when we were busy, it wasn't unusual to go the entire day without seeing the sun.

Sometime in the afternoon, I realized that Sebastian had been unusually silent all day. Normally, he would pipe up now and then with some acerbic comment or at least contribute to our conversations. I didn't recall hearing from him since last night, and the more I thought about it, that was right before Alex and I almost ripped each other's close off and humped one another in the sink. If that was the cause of Sebastian's sudden lack of communication, I needed to find out what his problem was.

"Yo, Sebastian."

Nothing.

"Sebastian, it's not like you can pretend you're not there."

I guess he could have been asleep; I never really considered his resting habits before, I just assumed that he slept when I slept. *Did he even have to sleep?* In any case, even if he was napping, we needed to talk.

"SEBASTIAN!

Once again, only silence. Exasperated, I blurted, "If you're not going to talk, then you're definitely going to listen."

I sounded remarkably parental, all I needed was to add "young man" and it could have been my mother talking. That was enough to make me change my tone, along with briefly considering smacking myself repeatedly for letting my upbringing get the better of me.

"Okay, I can guess that you are upset because Alex and I almost … and then didn't … and you were thinking that, finally, you could release some of your pent-up sexual urges. But we aren't as adventurous as you, and just weren't comfortable doing it the first time with you in attendance."

"You believe that is the reason for my brooding?" he said finally.

"It's not?"

"Not even close, my dear. Alexander is like a son to me. It would be as uncomfortable for me to be part of such an event as it would for the two of you."

Huh. If that wasn't the reason, I was stumped. If he wasn't ticked off because he missed out on a three-way by-proxy, why was he so mad?

Suddenly, I had an epiphany. Maybe all the sexual innuendo throughout the weeks he shared my body had

149

less to do with his baser needs, and more to do with his feelings for me.

"Uh, Sebastian, you aren't jealous by any chance, are you?"

He let out a long sigh.

"No, not jealous. Envious. As you are aware, I have been with many, many women in my life. Most have lasted one, maybe two nights. Some have even been what I like to call 'serial one-nighters'— one-night stands that repeat over a number of years. There are even a few women with whom I have had longer associations, but never with any serious commitment, at least not on my part.

"But throughout all those liaisons, the multitude of sexual encounters, I have never experienced the kind of intimacy that I sensed between the two of you last night. Not the torrent of passion in the bath, but later, when you slept, chastely entwined. I have never awakened with a woman with whom I did not have sex the night before. In fact, I have rarely spent the entire night with any of my conquests. I have never given or received pleasure or comfort from mere physical contact. And yesterday, when I was able to feel what you were feeling, I realized how shallow I truly am."

It didn't happen often, but I was speechless. Any of the cliché-riddled comments one might turn to in such circumstances seemed so inadequate when Sebastian had just stripped himself bare emotionally. The pain in his voice made me want to cry. Just when I thought I understood the narcissistic bastard, he went and confused me with a touching and eloquent revelation of self-awareness.

The moments ticked by, and I knew I had to say something, even if it turned out to be stupid. All I could come up with was, "I'm so sorry." Then, we just sat there in silence, and I tried my best to let my emotions tell him what I couldn't find the words for— that what he'd confided was both beautiful and devastating, and I hoped he could allow himself to find someone with whom he could experience more than what he had throughout his long, lonely life.

That's how Alex found me sometime later, still sitting quietly on the sofa. Sebastian hadn't requested it, but this was something between the two of us. I didn't plan to mention any of what he had divulged to Alex.

"I think we finally know where Sebastian's body is being held," Alex announced. "It's at Otto's place in the Czech Republic. One of our Eastern European informants passed along the information yesterday, and we confirmed it a few moments ago."

Finally. "That's fantastic! When do we leave?"

"Tomorrow. We'll fly commercial out of Boston direct to Reykjavik using our real passports. That way, if Otto is paying attention, he will think we are checking out his Icelandic residence. We'll take a private jet and use false documentation to get to Czech."

Not that I thought Boston was some Podunk town, but I was amazed that we wouldn't have to depart from New York's JFK airport.

"There's actually a non-stop flight from Boston to Iceland?"

Alex chuckled softly and shook his head. "Leave it to you to focus on the itinerary. But, yes, Iceland Air has one. It leaves in the evening and we arrive the next morning."

He walked over to a small table near the staircase and picked up what looked like a leather-covered notebook. When he handed it to me, I saw that it was a zippered planner, but without pages. Inside was a passport and driver's license; both had my photo, but with the name "Callista McMasters". There were even a couple of credit cards. Thank heaven I wasn't Bertha.

"You people think of everything, don't you?"

"We certainly try. I'm going to need to confer with Sebastian for a while, so if there's anything you need to do that can't wait, you should probably take care of it now." His expression softened a bit and he added, "We'll have dinner and a chance to relax later, I promise."

The only thing pressing at that moment was my bladder, so I made a quick trip to the bathroom and then made myself comfortable on the couch while Alex and Sebastian went over the details for our trip.

I didn't mind their magical, non-verbal exchanges of information, although I had to admit, holding hands with Alex was probably the reason. I did make a point to look for any changes in Alex's demeanor that might indicate Sebastian was divulging the inner angst he'd shared with me. When I didn't notice anything out of the ordinary, I figured my original assumption—that he wanted it kept confidential—was correct.

Alex made good on his promise of dinner and relaxing, and we spent most of the rest of the evening watching movies and snuggling on the sofa. Now that I was about to embark on my first trans-continental trip, I wished that I had brought some nicer outfits, but Alex pointed out that bringing so few things meant I didn't need to waste a lot of time packing, which meant more time on the couch with him.

Alex excused himself a little before eleven to make a few more calls, and I went into the kitchen to finish the dishes from dinner. When everything was clean and put away, I turned out the lights and went to get ready for bed.

I didn't see Alex in the living room—he was probably in his room taking another call. I went to the bathroom, exiting with minty fresh breath, and clothed in the least alluring outfit I could find—grey fleece sweatpants and an oversized University of Arizona t-shirt that hung down almost to my knees. No reason to make things more difficult with anything but non-sexy nightwear.

Alex wasn't in his room, but under the covers in my bed, and he'd claimed the left side. Since as far back as I could remember, I'd always slept on the left of any mattress bigger than a twin. It was just a habit, so I started over to the opposite side. As I pulled back the covers, however, Alex stopped me.

"Wait," he said as he scooted over. "I was just warming it up for you."

He held up the covers over the spot he'd just vacated, and I moved around the bed and climbed in. The sheets were, indeed, warm and cozy, a far cry from the chilliness winter usually imparts to bedding.

I turned on my side toward him. Alex was propped on one elbow, contentment on his face as he gazed into my eyes.

"That is the most considerate thing anyone has ever done for me," I said softly. "I really don't deserve you."

He pulled me to him and brushed his lips against mine. "Sure you do," he murmured before intensifying the kiss. Rolling onto his back, he tucked me next to him, and for the second night in a row, I fell asleep happier than I had been in a long, long time.

That night, I had my recurring first-date-after-divorce dream. It was basically the same as always, except instead of getting into my own car, Alex drove up in the rented Taurus and gave me detailed instructions how to make a more effective Molotov cocktail.

~16~

All I wanted was a nice, warm shower and a real bed. Unfortunately, after the four-hour drive to Boston, and an almost three-hour wait until the six-hour flight to Reykjavik, it would be a while before I got either.

Once we went through immigration at the airport, we were immediately whisked away in a nondescript Audi with well-tinted windows for another ride to the nondescript airfield to await our jet to Czech. If I thought New Hampshire was too northerly for my taste, we were now just below the Arctic Circle. It wasn't much colder than it had been at the safe house, but it was almost ten a.m. and still dark. Even when the sun finally rose, I couldn't really enjoy the view of the Icelandic countryside because it never got much brighter than twilight. The only thing that could make me any crankier was if Angelica turned out to be our pilot.

My day improved when I was introduced to Sigbjörn, an affable fellow who flew us to somewhere in Norway, where we changed planes and pilots—again, thankfully not Angelica—and jetted to some place in Poland. From there, we were driven into Czech, to the city of Pardubice, west of the capital, Prague. Once safely ensconced in a house that belonged to a local *Xyzok*, I finally got my shower—a mere twenty-two hours later.

"Was all that extra travel and plane changing necessary?" I complained, sitting down at the kitchen table. Alex shoved a plate of something that resembled a pale chicken-fried steak with creamy gravy and boiled potatoes in front of me.

"Better safe than sorry," he insisted, loading up a dish for himself. "We want Otto to think we're still in Iceland. To further promote that ruse, two *Xyzok* who resemble us checked into a hotel near Otto's place, and not flying directly makes us harder to track if he figures out they are impostors."

All that made sense and, after all, this kind of thing is what Alex and Sebastian did for a living. I felt bad that he might think I doubted his skills.

I tried some of the food, decided I liked it despite the monochromatic color scheme, and proceeded to consume every bit. Alex ate all his as well, but not with the same gusto that I had.

"So, what's next?" I asked, taking both our plates to rinse them in the sink.

"Dessert." He brought out a plate of small, rectangular pastries topped with whipped cream.

"I meant tomorrow." I eyed the seemingly open-faced cream puffs. "What are these?"

He popped one into his mouth. "Rakvička. It means, 'little coffins'."

"Let's hope that's not prophetic," I said, frowning. "But omens of misfortune aside, what's the plan?"

"Tomorrow, we find Sebastian's body and get his essence back where it belongs. I'll fill you in on the details in the morning."

Alex rose from the table, took my hand, and guided me out of the kitchen. "But, tonight, we get a good night's sleep. We will both need to be well rested for this to work."

My head barely touched the pillow before I was out. Generally, I'd never go to bed so soon after a heavy meal, but figured I would throw caution to the wind. I might be dead come tomorrow.

Alex may have slept in the same bed as I did—the other side looked rumpled when I awoke—but I couldn't say for certain. Either way, I did feel much better rested and in a more positive mood than the day before.

Over breakfast, Alex made good on his promise to provide the specifics for the day's activities. Otto had Sebastian's body on Kunětice Mountain, in a centuries-old castle located about four or five miles away. The mountaintop building was destroyed in the seventeenth century, and remained in ruin until the early nineteen-hundreds when restoration began. It took seventy-odd years to finish, and now it was open to the public.

Otto liked the location for the same reason it was so popular when it was built in the fourteen- hundreds; the landscape surrounding it was flat for miles in every direction, affording an excellent view of anyone trying to catch the inhabitants unawares. Using magic, he obscured himself from the tourists and security personnel when in residence. This type of squatting was, according to Sebastian, a common occurrence until about fifty years before, when it was banned, mostly because some humans could sense a Courso presence and thought their homes or businesses were haunted.

Local *Xyzok* operatives determined that Otto was currently away, with only a small contingent of his staff remaining. Being Courso, Alex would be able to interact with the building as it existed in its connection to the other dimension—he would see the castle as Otto would see it, not as a human would. After the castle closed for the night, we'd sneak in and find Sebastian's body. Then Alex, who over the last weeks had taken great pains to learn everything there was to know about spiritual convergence, would reconverge him. Alex and Sebastian made it sound like it would be easy, and I wasn't sure if that's really what they thought, or if they were trying to spare me the dangerous details. I was nervous enough, so not sharing any of their own apprehension was probably a good call.

By the time evening finally rolled around, I felt like I had downed a pot of coffee and a six-pack of Red Bull. My heart pounded, and when sitting still, I couldn't stop tapping my foot in jittery anticipation. To add to my overall discomfort, my hair was completely out of control and I had forgotten the damned hair sticks in New Hampshire. I was a jumble of nerves *and* looked like a crazed harpy.

Sebastian sensed my unease. *"It is normal to be anxious before a mission. In fact, it helps keep one sharp."*

"I suppose, but this is all way beyond my normal comfort zone," I complained, pacing across the room.

"I have done this hundreds of times. Trust me, my dear; you will feel more composed once we start doing something productive."

***

When evening fell, we drove to a village near the castle. The Czech people must have an aversion to vowels, as many of the words I'd seen on street signs and such seemed to be completely devoid of them. When I commented on the consonant-richness of the language, Alex explained that there was a common Czech tongue twister that meant, "stick a finger through your throat," that contained no vowels—*Strč prst skrz krk*. Sebastian offered, *plch pln skvm prch skrz drn prv zhlt čtvrt hrst zrn*, which translated meant, "A door mouse full of stains escaped through grass after first eating a quarter-handful of grain." I had no clue what that was supposed to mean, but Alex wrote them out for me so that I could fully appreciate the economic use of letters and sounds.

Such was the case with the name of the small town we were now in. Srch only had about nine-hundred inhabitants, but it did have its own public library, which was open only one day a week, Friday. As this was Wednesday, we were able to use it to meet up with our *Xyzok* backup, which consisted of six beefy, well-armed men, dressed as we were, all in black. I was a little puzzled about the guns; I figured that Courso would use magic as a weapon. Alex explained that while magic can be effective against humans, its use is limited in the human dimension to avoid any witnesses having to be mind-purged afterward. Bullets generally move too fast to be magically countered, which would be helpful against Otto. It was also why all firearms were banned in *his* dimension.

Once everyone was clear on their part of the operation, we headed out to the castle, initially in cars, which were left near a restaurant below the mountain, then on foot. By Arizona standards, Kunětice Mountain was only a hill, so the trek to the castle, slow because we stayed off the road and didn't use flashlights, wasn't particularly strenuous.

At the top, Alex and I moved stealthily toward the castle, while our backups fanned out around the perimeter, but remained hidden. Their job was to make certain no one arrived unexpectedly while we were inside, and intervene only if Alex signaled for aid. If we required help, he'd contact them via a speed-dial text message to their cell phones. Low tech, but effective, apparently.

The hulking structure had minimal outside lighting, and while Alex and the others may have had the eyesight of cats, I sure as hell didn't. Absent a pair of night-vision goggles, the only way for me to keep up was to stay close to Alex and hope I didn't fall on my ass.

Silently, Alex and I circled around to the far end of the castle. He began to run his fingertips lightly along the stones of the turret, then stopped, the electrical buzz of magic wafting from him in waves. Then, he walked through the wall. In truth, he found the previously invisible doorway and walked through that, but the optics were awesome, nonetheless.

It wasn't a certainty that I, being human, would be able to pass through. However, Sebastian believed his powerful essence would override that hurdle. As I moved closer, all I could see was Alex's hand jutting out from a hazy, dark area amongst the blocks.

"I don't think this is going to work, I whispered."

"It is alright, my dear. Go ahead," Sebastian urged. *"I am almost never wrong, after all."*

It was the "almost" that scared me, but the worst that would happen was I'd smack into the wall, and we'd have to find another way in.

Moving cautiously, relief swept over me when my hand slid through the stones as if they weren't there. We'd agreed that the less magic used, the less likely our presence would be detected. Alex had to conjure up some to allow us to enter Otto's hideaway, but because Sebastian generated a fair amount of magical energy when he spoke in my head, it would be safest if he kept quiet once we were inside the castle. This meant I was spared the inevitable, "I told you so," when his theory proved correct, but I could feel his grating self-satisfaction despite the silence.

I walked forward, and found myself at the beginning of a long, dark passageway. As difficult as navigating outside had been, I hadn't realized the how much light the distant city provided until enveloped by the utter blackness inside the castle walls. Disoriented by the lack of visual cues, I grabbed Alex's hand to keep my bearings.

"I only sense three live signatures here—all unknown to me, but none are particularly powerful," Alex whispered. "Probably just a nominal crew left to oversee the premises while Otto is not in residence."

"Live signatures? As opposed to dead ones?"

"Well, all Courso leave some lingering evidence of themselves even when they are no longer present. There are many residuals here; including Otto's. I am aware of only three Courso. That's what I meant by 'live'."

We continued walking for what seemed like forever. In reality, it was probably only minutes, but I've never been especially patient under the best of circumstances, and this was anything but. At least I became more accustomed to the pitch black. What had been a soul-sucking void was now merely hella-dark.

When the tunnel forked, Alex stood perfectly still, much as he had before he found the doorway. After a moment, he lifted his head slightly and took a long, deep breath.

"I can smell Sebastian. We are very close, go to the right."

I'd witnessed the heightened sense of eyesight and hearing, and while Alex mentioned previously that the Coursodon enjoyed over-developed olfactory abilities, it didn't occur to me that meant he had a nose like a freaking bloodhound. *I'll bet that talent could be a problem when jammed in a crowded elevator on a hot, sweaty day.* Maybe I needed to tone down my use of scented bath products, as well.

Eventually, the corridor widened, a steep stairway along one side. With no railing and narrow, uneven treads, we ascended with caution, pressed against the wall for added safety. At the top was a wooden door, through which was a landing and another staircase. The pattern continued with two more doors and stairways until we found ourselves before a much larger, and more ornate, carved door. It was locked, but Alex touched just above the levered handle and the door swung open.

Instead of the cramped, bleak passage, we were now standing in a high-ceilinged, elegantly decorated hallway, illuminated by the soft glow of dimmed wall sconces. I felt a little like Dorothy, as she opened the door from her black-and-white world, to the riot of colors in Oz. We definitely weren't in Kansas anymore—or, more precisely, Kunětice castle. Well, technically we were still in the castle, but this was the magically-created residence of Otto Kashanian, and the only reason that I, as a human, could perceive it was because I was harboring Sebastian. It boggled my mind to think about how many people had stood right where I was, but hadn't seen anything other than the ruined fortress.

We crept along, pausing occasionally for Alex to get his bearings. As we approached yet another door, my head was filled with Sebastian's soft groan. Alex mouthed a silent, "He's in there."

"There" turned out to be a sizeable room that, in an old English manor, might have been a parlor. Rich, dark, wood paneling covered the walls and ornate furnishings decorated the space. Directly in front of us was a huge stone fireplace, big enough for two or three people to stand in. To the left, spotlighted by recessed bulbs in the ceiling, was Sebastian.

I gasped, reflexively bringing my hand up to cover my mouth and hide my horror. Alex said something quietly, but harshly in Courso. I assumed it was profanity.

The body stood upright, eyes closed, in a curved, glass-fronted case. I couldn't tell how he was propped up in there—probably some kind of invisible, magical tethers at work. Several LED displays blinked on the front of the enclosure, monitoring the temperature and humidity levels inside. *Technology meets the supernatural,* I supposed.

I studied the electronic numbers. "The interior conditions are controlled. Can we get him out or will that harm him?"

"I doubt it, his body shouldn't decompose, but there's only one way to find out for sure."

Alex pulled open the front panel and we heard a small pop, like the sound of the vacuum breaking on a sealed jar. Despite Alex's reassurances, I was relieved when Sebastian didn't shrivel up or turn into a pile of ashes. I gingerly touched his hand; the flesh was cool, but otherwise felt surprisingly normal. As Alex grabbed Sebastian's shoulders and lifted, the body lost all its former rigidity and collapsed.

He laid Sebastian on the floor, and crouched next to him. As Alex's hand hovered over his mentor's torso, he murmured, "Fascinating, I can feel a slight energy surge. It's as if his corporeal-self knows his spiritual-essence is here."

The opposite was also true. Overwhelmed with Sebastian's rage, eagerness, and determination, it was difficult to keep his emotions in check, much less my own. It took all my concentration to retain some semblance of calm while Alex's floating hands continued the examination.

After many minutes, Alex dropped to his knees and let out a long breath. "Fortunately, everything is intact, and I have healed the damage that led to his death." He looked exhausted, and we hadn't even started the reconvergence.

"Do you need to take a break before we continue?" I asked.

"No, I'm fine. We should proceed; I don't want to be here any longer than we have to." He twined his fingers with mine. "You ready?"

"Let's do it," I replied emphatically.

"Hold Sebastian's hands and, whatever you do, don't let go."

Scooting next to Sebastian, I moved his hands to rest on his chest, then grasped them firmly. Alex positioned himself near Sebastian's head, placed his hands over mine and I felt the now familiar zing of magic. His head dropped and his body stiffened, and while the buzz increased steadily until it became painful, I held on tight.

The magic seemed to be coming into me from Alex, but was also flowing out of me with equal, if not greater, intensity. The discomfort intensified until my hands felt like they would burst into flames. Just when I thought I'd have to let go, the agony abruptly subsided.

I glanced at Alex; he slowly lifted his head, removed his hands, and looked expectantly at the still inert form before us. Suddenly, I felt movement under my hand, and let out a small, joyous yip when his fingers stretched.

Alex gazed at me with cautious anticipation before we both turned our attention back to Sebastian.

"His color looks more normal," I remarked when I realized his once pasty-gray complexion was becoming pinker. Alex touched Sebastian's forehead and reported that he was now much warmer as well.

A moment later, Sebastian's lids flitted open. "Thank you, Alexander," he said, his speech rough and hesitant. "Well done. And Hailey, my dear, lovely to finally see you through my own eyes."

His voice was quite different than the one I'd heard in my head all these weeks. I supposed the discrepancy was like how one perceives their own voice when hearing it on a recording.

"Can you sit up?" Alex asked, even as he began to lift his mentor's upper body off the floor. Sebastian was now more or less upright, but still weak. Alex kept a hand on his back to keep him from collapsing.

"I believe I shall require a few moments to recover before I can stand. But, as soon as possible, I would appreciate a very large scotch and a very rare steak."

Just then, all the lights came on and a deep voice drifted across the room.

"Sorry *Xyzok*, but we are all out just now."

~17~

Before I could register that we were no longer alone, two unpleasant looking men carrying really, really, big guns surrounded us.

Alex raised his hands, so I did, too. Sebastian didn't move, but he must not have looked like much of a threat, because the gunmen ignored him. Another man, who I assumed was the owner of the voice, moved between them and surveyed us with a cruel smile.

"Ah, so nice of you to visit. I see you found Sebastian; I'm sure he must be delighted to be reconnected with his body." Sneering, he stared at me and said, "I have yet to make the acquaintance of this lovely young woman—I am Otto Kashanian. And you must be Hailey."

Yep, definitely the source of the bass. Alex stood very slowly, never taking his eyes off the men with the guns.

"She's no concern of yours, Otto. You have us. Let her go."

"Now, now, what's the fun in that? Besides, I am the captor, and as such, I get to decide what happens to the captives."

He laughed as he spoke, but his dark eyes showed nothing but malice. Otto was lean but not well muscled, and not particularly tall—perhaps only an inch or two bigger than I was. He wasn't particularly good looking either, but his auburn hair was short and neat, and he wore a suit that fit him like it was made for him. Which it probably was, since, according to Alex and Sebastian, he'd amassed a sizable fortune from his criminal activities.

Otto nodded at his lackeys and one lowered his gun and frisked us, taking our cell phones. *Great*, I thought, as he handed them to Otto, *there goes our ability to let the others know we're in trouble.*

As Lackey One moved back to his original position, I noticed a curved pattern tattooed on his left hand. Upon further study, I realized that Lackey Two had the same tat. That explained the guy asking Wyatt questions; I wondered if all Otto's minions were so marked. Must be something new or Alex and Sebastian would have recognized it from Wyatt's description.

Otto walked across the room and sat behind a large, intricately carved mahogany desk. He lifted the receiver of an old-school rotary telephone and spoke in a neutral tone.

"Edita, I am hungry. I'll have that Kung Pao now." He looked out at us. "Would any of you like anything?" When none of us answered, he shrugged. "No? Just the Kung Pao then."

He hung up, moved around to the front of the desk, and leaned casually against its edge, feet crossed at the ankles and arms crossed over his chest.

"I have forgotten my manners. There's no reason for you to be uncomfortable. Please, come sit." He gestured to a red velvet-covered settee positioned opposite of where he stood.

When none of us moved, Lackey One prodded us towards the couch with the barrel of his gun. Alex and I helped Sebastian, who was still unable to stand—much less walk—carefully propping him up with some throw pillows against one side of the sofa. He was still listing to one side, but at least he remained upright. I settled down in the middle, while Alex sat on the far end.

"You knew we were coming and masked your signature, didn't you?" Alex asked, making no attempt to hide the venom in his voice. "Who set us up?"

Otto smirked. "All in good time. Suffice it to say, it was no secret you were searching for Kess and I decided to lure you here by letting it be known where his body was located. So simple and yet so effective, don't you think? And now, here you are, as planned."

There was a small rap on the door. "Come," he bellowed.

A plump woman, her graying hair pulled back in an elaborate bun, entered. She carried a tray loaded with covered dishes, a teapot, and two small cups without handles. She arranged the tray on the desk, uncovered the bowls, and poured some tea into one of the cups.

Otto gazed at the food, joyfully rubbed his hands together and exclaimed, "There's nothing like Edita's Kung Pao Chicken. She makes it better than any place in China. Eastern European food tends to be so bland, but she knows how to use peppers."

Without uttering a word, Edita retreated from the room. Otto tucked a starched, white cloth napkin into his collar and snatched one of the bowls along with a set of elaborately decorated gold chopsticks. He placed the bowl up to his chin and deftly manipulated the sticks. As he shoveled in the first mouthful, his eyes closed and he moaned a breathy, "Exquisite."

"Why did you keep Sebastian's body?" Alex asked.

"Well," Otto answered while he continued to chew, "I keep all my best kills. I have them in all my homes. They provide me with such warm memories of my triumphs over my enemies." He looked directly at me. "Enemies vex me so."

When Otto finished his food, he yanked the napkin from his neck and daintily dabbed his mouth with it. He set the bowl and napkin back on the tray and took a swig of tea. Then, he motioned to the two gunmen, who left the room. Their departure made me feel less tense—now that automatic weapons weren't pointed at us, maybe the situation wasn't completely hopeless.

Otto must have noticed some change in my expression or the set of my shoulders, because he wagged his index finger at me and clucked in admonishment, "I had Petr and Enrique leave because they do not need to be privy to this sensitive information. But don't get any ideas. Even without them, the odds are still decidedly in my favor. You are human, weak, and slow. Poor Sebastian here is in no condition to do much of anything. Thus, the only danger to me is Alex, but I believe he too is a bit depleted from his expenditure of energy when restoring his mentor."

He moved back around the desk and opened the center drawer. "Besides," he said, grinning widely as he pulled out a small, dark handgun and pointed it at me. "If Alex moves, I'll shoot *you*."

I gulped reflexively and glanced at Alex. He reached over, squeezed my hand, and then inclined his head at Otto to assure him he had no plans to endanger me.

"Now, where was I? Oh yes," Otto continued, "all my other trophies just stand there, lifeless, as one might expect. But Sebastian was different. I suppose that shouldn't have surprised me; he was always unique. His body still seemed to have just the tiniest stirrings of life, just a whisper of energy that didn't diminish. Quite amazing, really."

Otto sat down in the desk chair, keeping the pistol aimed at me. "Of course, this anomaly piqued my curiosity. I knew the *Xyzok* would try to locate the body—they always like a proper send off for the dearly departed—and you, Alex, were the most likely one to lead the search. I had my people keep an eye on you. I must say, your skills as an investigator are decidedly overrated, considering how long it took you to unravel the mystery. I was beginning to doubt whether you would ever provide any useful information at all. But then, during a casual discussion with a colleague concerning the demise of the dear *Xyzok*, he mentioned that he didn't realize Sebastian had a sister."

Otto leaned toward us slightly and continued in a stage whisper, "It seems he noticed you two in Arizona and recognized the signature. He naturally assumed that she must be his sister."

He pushed back in the chair and looked thoughtfully at me for a moment. "I checked, and indeed, Sebastian has no siblings. I also discovered that you are quite human, no Courso blood at all."

I recalled the story we had told at the safe house, and I felt compelled to ask, "Why didn't you assume I was pregnant with Sebastian's baby?"

"I did entertain that as a reasonable explanation, but I quickly determined that you and he had never been closer than the same continent during the last year. Even considering Sebastian's *purported* extraordinary prowess with women, I concluded that couldn't be the source of his signature within you."

Sebastian snorted derisively. Typical—even completely drained of energy and being held by a psycho-hoodlum, his ego kicked in. As I looked closer, however, I noticed that he did look a little perkier than before.

Maybe Sebastian would regain his strength and along with Alex, the two of them would save the day. Probably just grasping at straws—Sebastian may have looked a bit better, but he still was obviously a long way from being able to help take down Otto. Now that I looked more carefully at Alex, Otto was right; he wasn't looking all that great either.

Otto ignored Sebastian and went on with his monologue. "Then, I recalled hearing that Sebastian had some long-standing interest in reconvergence and I began to wonder if he had somehow achieved what before had only been conjecture—had he actually transferred his spiritual-self to another? But it wasn't until you and the girl got to Pardubice that I was certain. The closer you got to the castle, the more energy the body emitted—as though it was calling out to itself. I couldn't quite resolve the apparent conundrum of how Sebastian ended up in this human—if he hadn't been close enough to impregnate her, how could he possess her? I trust you will be able to clear that up for me, yes?"

The phone on the desk chimed once. Otto answered, listened for a moment and said, "Excellent. Send our guest in." He placed the gun on the desk when the door opened, but from my position on the sofa, I couldn't see who had entered. Alex, however, was angled so that he was facing the door, and his eyes narrowed when he caught sight of the newcomer.

"I believe you all know Angelica," Otto announced proudly.

I swiveled around to get a look. It was, indeed, Angelica. This time, instead of her sedate pilot uniform, she had on a cream-colored, clingy sweater with a neckline cut low to display her ample breasts and a hem cut high to expose her sculpted abs. The outfit was finished off with similarly colored super-tight pants tucked into knee-high, stiletto-heeled boots.

She crossed the room slowly, glancing at us briefly as she swept past. When she reached the desk, she dropped into Otto's lap and kissed him with great enthusiasm.

"That fucking, traitorous bitch," I hissed under my breath.

Sebastian forced out a ragged, "Indeed."

When Otto and the Demon Skank from Hell finally came up for air, Alex's voice vibrated with barely controlled rage.

"Angelica, you took an oath to defend the laws of Courso. What is your explanation for this treachery?"

"I've grown weary of working long hours transporting people less intelligent than I for little pay and no chance for advancement." She traced a finger lazily over Otto's lips. "Otto made me a better offer."

Alex shook his head. "How long has this been going on?"

Otto began speaking before Angelica had a chance to respond. *Jeez, that guy likes to hear himself talk.*

"Oh, for a year or so. You will also be pleased to know that she was instrumental in supplying the information that allowed me to ambush and kill Sebastian." A contemptuous grin spread over Otto's lips. "Or, at least, I believed I killed him."

He turned to look directly at Sebastian. "I watched the life fade from your eyes, *Xyzok*. I don't completely understand how you managed it, much less how you ended up inside this human, but the ability to transfer one's spiritual-self into another is like discovering the mythical fountain of youth. Those who desire immortality will certainly pay anything to obtain it. That is why I lured Alex here. I will know how it works, and I will be rich beyond even my expectations."

Sebastian struggled to straighten himself without much success. He took a deep breath and sputtered, "Never."

Angelica laughed and disengaged herself from Otto's embrace. Standing in front of the desk, she purred, "I don't think you are in much of a position to say no. Tell us, or the human will suffer for your refusal."

She glared at me, pure hatred etched upon her overly made-up face. "Truly, I hope he doesn't give us the details right away. I will enjoy the pain I inflict upon you."

I was pretty sure she wasn't just grandstanding to get Sebastian and Alex to give them the information. She was looking forward to torturing me.

My stomach churned. I was terrified, but I'd be damned if I was going to let her know it. Besides, if I did vomit, I was so doing it on her and, at the moment, she was too far away to accomplish that goal.

"You keep your hands off her," Alex growled. "The process is not like a recipe for a cake. We can teach you, but it will take time."

"Alexander," Sebastian cautioned. "Don't."

"I won't sacrifice her for this."

Somehow, I didn't think telling Otto what he wanted to know was going to keep me—or Alex and Sebastian for that matter—safe. It might prolong the inevitable, but I couldn't see how this was going to end well for any of us.

I looked over at Sebastian. He still seemed very weak—his lids were closed, his breathing shallow. As I placed my hand on his forehead to check if he was too hot or cold, his eyes opened, and he stared into mine. I'm not sure how I understood what he wanted me to do—maybe the weeks of inter-body cohabitation left us with some peculiar ability for wordless communication. In any case, I knew he wasn't nearly as debilitated as he appeared. Not anywhere near a hundred percent, however, and he and Alex needed a diversion to have any chance at overtaking both Otto and Angelica.

And that diversion was me.

The easiest way to overcome incapacitating, gut-wrenching fear is by doing something completely insane. At least, that's how it seemed to me. Perhaps it was having something to do besides just sit there and listen to two sociopaths prattle on, but I felt much less fear now that I had an assignment.

Otto and Alex were trying to iron out the details of the best way for the secrets of deconvergence to be divulged. Alex was sticking with his initial contention that it would take more than an abridged version, but Otto was not completely convinced. However, he was so obsessed with being able to sell virtual immortality—not to mention being able to attain it for himself—that he wasn't protesting too vociferously. I was positive that Alex had no intention of telling him anything he would find useful, and hoped that somehow these negotiations were part of Sebastian's plan.

I took a deep breath and stood up. Angelibitch watched me, not with wariness—she obviously saw me as no threat—more the way a not-too-hungry lioness might regard a crippled gazelle.

I gestured to the teapot. "May I?"

"Certainly," she answered. "I don't plan on drinking any."

I poured myself a cup of tea, took a sip, and leaned on the edge of the desk near where Devilica was perched.

"You know, I really don't see the attraction."

She glanced at Otto, still negotiating with Alex and Sebastian. "What he lacks in looks, he more than makes up for with his riches."

"Oh, that's not what I meant. I can't figure out why so many men are so hot for you. You're attractive in an off-the-strip, cheap, Vegas titty-bar kind of way, but really, aren't guys put off by the fact that there's probably no one they know or may meet in the future that hasn't already banged you?"

Her eyes narrowed to tiny slits. "Look cunt, I would kill you now if Otto didn't want you alive. But know this— when Otto gets the information he wants, I will kill you … and slowly."

I smiled brightly and continued as though she hadn't threatened me.

"Well, I may die, but at least I can make myself feel better by letting you know that after you flew us to New Hampshire, Alex spent the next night making fun of you. What did he say exactly? Oh, I remember, he said you were as adventurous in bed as a sloth and he only fucked you because you begged him." I figured if she could use the c-word, dropping the f-bomb was entirely appropriate.

Alex had told me that the Coursodon were faster than humans, but Angelica's fist landed on my chin so quickly, I didn't even see her move. The punch propelled me back onto the desk, she leapt on top of me and wrapped her hands around my throat.

Angelica wasn't saying anything, but the pure, unadulterated rage on her face spoke volumes. I couldn't get any air, but saw Otto try to pry her off me. *Don't want to lose your control over Alex, do you, asshole?*

As he grabbed her arms, I noticed a flash of movement to my left and felt immediate relief as Angelica released her grip on my neck. I was in a lot of pain, and rolled onto my side get my breath. From that position, I saw Alex landing kidney punches to Otto's back while Sebastian grappled with Angelica.

Under normal circumstances, the She-Bitch would be no match for Sebastian, but his recent reconvergence had evened the playing field considerably. She pulled free and smashed a lamp across his face, causing him to stagger and fall to one knee. At the same time, Otto twisted away from Alex, grabbed the gun from the desk, and leveled it at Alex.

The sound of the gunshots thundered in my head. I lifted myself up and watched in horror as Alex collapsed backwards, blood spilling out from the center of his chest.

"No!" I screamed.

No, no, no. Not Alex—he has to be okay, I thought frantically. As I tried to crawl to where he was sprawled on the floor, Angelica grabbed my hair and yanked me upright.

Shoving me onto the desk, I fell, face-first, near the remnants of Otto's food, overturned in the melee. My hand landed next to the fancy chopsticks and I palmed one just as Angelica barked menacingly, "You're dead."

She flipped me over and pulled me up by the front of my shirt; the momentum helped propel the chopstick toward her. I wasn't aiming for any particular spot, but she leaned her head in—probably intending to taunt me again before she killed me—which allowed me to ram the pointy end of the make-shift weapon directly into her left eye.

I expected her to scream. Instead, she stood silent and motionless, one hand still clutching my shirt. Only a few inches of the chopstick protruded from her ruined eye and blood oozed freely from the now mostly empty socket. I felt her grip relax, her knees buckled, and she slid to the floor.

I wanted to heave, and probably would have had not Otto picked that moment to shoot me. The sound was deafening and searing pain erupted in my shoulder. He pointed the gun at me again, but Sebastian launched himself at his legs, causing Otto to tumble backward. The second shot whizzed over my head.

With Otto now on the floor, Sebastian leapt upon him. He grabbed the gun still clutched in Otto's hand, trying desperately to find the strength to wrestle it free. Sebastian was tiring, though, and before I could think of a way to help, Otto had pushed him away.

Not wanting Sebastian to be shot, I jumped, landing with both feet on Otto's wrist, dislodging the gun from his grip. I then kicked the weapon as far away as possible.

Eyes filled with rage, Otto stood and came at me. He grabbed my shoulders, and screeching like a wounded animal, flung me viciously across the room. I hit the big stone fireplace with such force, I heard the snap of bones breaking.

Intense, unyielding agony enveloped me. I heard a crash, a lot of yelling, and everything went black.

~18~

I heard lively, high-pitched twitters that sounded like sparrows or finches arguing over seed in a bird feeder. *Does Otto have an aviary?*

Wherever I was, it was dark. *Maybe I'm dreaming? Dead?* I concentrated on forcing my lids open. *That's better—there's some light. I must have just had my eyes closed.* While my eyes were now open, everything was blurry. Blinking a few times made things finally come into focus.

I was in a bed. A big bed—king sized, with a fancy antique brass canopy. That was probably a good sign. Hospitals only had twin beds and the closest thing to a canopy was the privacy screen hung from the ceiling. I couldn't see a clock anywhere, but filtered light came through a large bay window, so it was likely either just after dawn or just before sunset. Tilting my head to the side, I took in my surroundings: a spacious room, appointed with lots of nice furniture. There was also an IV trailing from one arm.

Shifting my head to the opposite side, I noticed a woman slouched in a large, upholstered chair next to the bed. She was sleeping, and her long, dark hair partially obscured her face, making identification impossible. As if the mystery woman sensed I was staring at her, she lifted her head, and her features came into horrifying focus.

Angelica.

She bolted out of the chair toward me. I screamed and tried to get out of bed, but my body wasn't cooperating. Surprisingly, Angelica stopped, gazed at me with an odd, agonized expression, and pleaded, "It's not what you think!"

Really? I was thinking that since I shoved a chopstick in your eye, you're probably more pissed at me than when you just wanted to kill me for no apparent reason. Actually, her eye looked a little odd, but not destroyed the way I remembered it.

I was still shrieking when Sebastian ran into the room. Instead of grabbing Angelica and pummeling her, he said, "Don't be afraid, it's all right," to me, and, "move away," to Angelica. She complied, backing into a corner.

Sebastian sat on the edge of the bed and gently grasped my hand. "I am sorry, my dear. If we had realized you were set to awaken, I would have made sure it was I you saw first."

"What the fuck is she doing here?" I shouted frantically. "And where is Alex?"

Sebastian and Angelica glanced at each other, and she dropped her head.

I felt a warm tingling where Sebastian's and my hands touched that quickly spread throughout my body. It must have been one of those Courso anti-anxiety specials, because I immediately felt more composed.

I gave him the stink-eye. "Did you just drug me?"

"Forgive me, but I have much to tell you and it will be much easier for you if you are less agitated."

I *was* calmer, and thinking more clearly. All sorts of things were now running through my mind. Was Sebastian in cahoots with Angelica, playing Alex and me the whole time? Or was this Otto, making himself look like

Sebastian? "The Courso can alter their appearance, you could be anyone."

Sebastian gazed at me intently. "You are employed by a maker of chinchilla-milk cheese."

Not common knowledge, but not exactly a secret either.

"Not good enough," I said, shaking my head.

A small smile curved on his lips. "You keep your underwear in the middle drawer of your dresser, arranged by color like the spectrum, with black next to purple and white on the opposite end by red."

"True, but if someone interrogated Wyatt, someone could have broken into my house, too. I'm still not convinced you are Sebastian."

"Once you realized that I could see what you could, you never undressed without closing your eyes except for one time, on my birthday, when you let me peek at you in the full-length mirror."

He had me there. Much as I tried, I couldn't think of any way someone other than my former body-mate could know that. I never even told Alex that I self-flashed Sebastian to commemorate his two-hundred and forty-sixth.

"Okay, I believe you're really you. But you'd better explain everything that happened after I passed out, because I'm still not completely sure I can trust you."

Sebastian smiled. "I have betrayed neither you nor Alexander, but I am pleased that you are wary given the circumstances. Now, do you want your explanation told chronologically, which I must say I prefer, or in some other format of your own choosing?"

"Damn you, Sebastian!" I took a deep breath before I asked the most important question, the one I needed the answer to most. "Is Alex alive?"

Sebastian looked over at Angelica. "Yes."

The vise grip that had been clenched on my heart finally let loose and my eyes welled with tears. After taking a moment to compose myself, I said, "Where is he? Why isn't he here?"

"Hailey, I *am* here."

But it wasn't Alex that said those words—it came from the bitch skulking across the room.

I looked at Sebastian with a combination of confusion and anger. "What the hell is she talking about?"

"Immediately after you hit the fireplace, our backup rushed in. They heard the gunfire and knew something was wrong, but had to take out the hired guns before they could get to us. In any event, Otto was arrested and the area secured. The instant they entered the room, I went to Alexander."

Sebastian paused, a wince flitted briefly over his face.

"He was gravely injured—two gunshot wounds to the chest, significant damage to a number of organs. I tried to heal him, but was too exhausted from the reconvergence and the fight, and was not certain that even at my best the damage could be repaired. I knew he was fading. You had conveniently dispatched Angelica, her spiritual essence had dissipated and her wounds, while fatal, were more easily repaired. Therefore, I healed Angelica's body and transferred Alexander to her."

I heard all the words, but I couldn't quite wrap my head around it. After what seemed like an hour, but was probably only a few moments, Angelica… uh, Alex, slowly moved toward the bed, stopping a few feet from the footboard.

My voice was small and quavering when I could finally form words. I studied the person before me, but saw no trace of the man I knew. "Is it really you?"

"Yes. I'm so sorry you were frightened."

"We were concerned, and apparently rightly so," Sebastian interrupted, shooting a dirty look toward Alex, "that if you saw Alexander in his current state, without prior explanation, you might have a negative reaction. However, he has not left your side since you were brought here. In fact, he refused to leave until he was certain that you were alright."

The tears that I'd held in check flowed freely now. I buried my head in my hands and sobbed, relieved that Alex was alive, but bewildered as to what this all meant. When all the pent-up anxiety, fear, and confusion had dissipated, I stopped crying and wiped my face with a corner of the bed sheet.

Finally, I asked, "How long have I been here, and for that matter, where is here?"

"You're in a *Xyzok* safe house in Prague," Sebastian replied. "You were pretty banged up. In addition to the relatively minor gunshot wound to your shoulder, your aerial adventure, courtesy of Otto, added a severe concussion, a compound fracture of your arm, and several broken ribs."

My body felt kind of rubbery, but nothing seemed to hurt. I lifted my arms and examined them; they both worked fine and neither had a cast, but the one without the IV did have a gauze bandage wrapped about halfway between my wrist and elbow.

"I must have been unconscious for a long time, I don't feel any pain."

Alexelica answered this time. "About three days. We sent for the best healers in this part of Europe, your wounds healed while you were still out. I was so worried when you didn't wake up right away. The healers said it was unpredictable because you were human."

I could barely look her ... him ... in the eye, one of which I vividly remembered popping like a bubble tea-pearl in a Vietnamese fruit drink. Not wanting to dwell on the fact that I'd killed someone, I forced myself to think of something else.

"What did you mean, Sebastian, when you said he refused to leave?"

"We attempted to repair Alexander's corporeal-self, but have not been able to do so; there is extensive damage to his heart. However, the most skilled healers are quite old and refuse to travel to this dimension. I am hopeful that they will have more success, but it will require Alexander to travel with his body and the sooner we start, the better. However, he would not budge whilst he felt you were in any danger."

"I thought it was impossible for an empty body to cross dimensions without disintegrating."

Sebastian patted my hand. "True, but we are almost positive if Alexander's corporeal-self crosses in close physical proximity to his spiritual-self, there will be no danger."

"Almost positive?" I looked impatiently back and forth between Sebastian and the perfidious cow formerly known as Angelica. "Don't you think waiting until you are positive would be preferable?"

Sebastian didn't answer right away. Instead, he looked over at Alexelica, who let out a breath and nodded, then turned to stare out the window.

"I wish we had the time to be absolutely certain. But, as you know, this is not an exact science." Sebastian ran a hand through his hair. "Truth be told, it is not even a science at all. This obviously has never been tried, but his spiritual-self will be right there with his corporeal-self. Based on how my body reacted when in proximity to my essence within you, I believe that Alexander's will be protected by his essence in Angelica if they cross together."

He paused before continuing. "I do not want to risk Alexander with my ignorance. At the moment, he appears to be safe where he is. However, he insists on having his own body—a desire I understand completely—so I will do whatever I can. Even if his body survives the crossing, that is only the first hurdle. As I said before, his corporeal-self has extensive damage that, even with healing, may not be able to sustain life. It is, after all, not the usual practice to restore a body once the spirit has died, so again, it is foreign territory."

"Are you saying if Alex makes it past the crossing, he could die during the reconvergence?"

"I am saying that I do not know. The only examples of successful transference I have to build upon are me into you, and now Alexander into Angelica. There are many differences between the two situations: I indirectly broadcast myself into a human host that was alive, while Alexander is now the sole inhabitant in Angelica's body. And transferring Alexander back to Alexander will be unique as well."

A young girl came into the room. Of course, she was probably Courso, so "young" was a relative term. She looked about seventeen, but was probably in her seventies. She carried one of those trays with the legs for eating in bed, which she placed on a dresser across the room. Sebastian moved from the side of the bed as she approached.

"I'm glad to see you awake," she said cheerfully, rearranging the pillows behind me and helping me sit up.

She retrieved the tray and set it over my outstretched legs. There was some kind of clear soup and a bottle of water. I took a swig of the water; it was cool and, thankfully, noncarbonated, and felt fantastic trickling down my dry throat.

"You should try to eat some broth," the girl coaxed. "If you can keep that down, we can move to solid food. But you haven't eaten in three days, so it's best to take it slow."

The soup smelled good, but I wasn't hungry—just twitchy and a little nauseated. Apparently, there was way too much potential for disaster with regard to Alex for either my psyche or stomach to handle. Still, I knew she was right, and that I needed to have at least a little.

I loaded the spoon with the dark liquid and took a tentative sip. Not only was it delicious, but it seemed to immediately settle the queasiness. Suddenly overwhelmed with hunger, I wondered if someone spiked my food with a magical anti-emetic or appetite enhancer. Whatever the reason for my newfound hunger, I finished every drop. I was still consumed with worry, but physically, I felt better.

Sebastian crossed the room and stood next to Alexelica.

"We have tarried too long, my boy. I'm sure you two would like a few moments alone and I have some details to attend to before we depart." Sebastian placed a reassuring hand on his shoulder before departing.

Neither of us said anything at first, we just looked at each other. I've always hated awkward silences, so finally I reached my hand out toward Alexelica. He—she?—took it hesitantly at first, then grasped it in both of his. Or hers. Shit, I was confused.

I studied the person in front of me. Gone were the sexy clothes and expertly applied makeup. Instead, this was the scrubbed clean version of Angelica, with hair pulled back in a simple braid and dressed in a pair of jeans and an oversized sweatshirt. The eyes that stared into mine were icy-blue, not Alex's rich cornflower, and again I tried to find something of him in her face. Finally, I saw it; the expression of concern mixed with affection was definitely all Alex.

"Just when I thought this whole situation couldn't get any weirder, now I find out you're transsexual," I joked, feebly trying to break the tension.

He smiled and shook his head. "Leave it to you to find something amusing in all this."

"Hey, you should know by now that when I get nervous, I can't control the smart-ass."

"It is one of your most endearing qualities."

Now that I had let out some of my tension with snark, I could be serious. "Alex, are you sure you want to risk going back to Courso?"

"Yes. I want to return to my own body."

"Okay, I'll come with you."

"I wish you could, but only those with magic can move between dimensions. You might have been able to when you harbored Sebastian, but it will be impossible now. Look, I won't be able to communicate with you directly once I cross, but I will come back, I promise, one way or another."

I really hadn't come to grips yet with the possible ramifications of Alex permanently inhabiting Angelica, and now wasn't the time to talk about it. I said simply, "We'll figure it out."

Sebastian came back into the room, followed by Opie and Mr. Mochaccino, our contacts in the desert when we left Arizona.

"Aiden and Cortez will stay here until you are able to travel, and then will escort you back to Tucson," Sebastian announced. Then he turned to Alexelica and said, "It is time."

Alex squeezed my hand again, leaned down, and placed a gentle kiss on my forehead. He took a long look at me—one I hoped wouldn't be the last—and walked out the door with Sebastian.

Tears spilled onto my cheeks as I stared at the empty doorway. Aiden and Cortez excused themselves, muttering something about going to check on someone somewhere else.

Finally alone, I let loose and buried my head in my hands, sobbing until no tears remained.

~19~

Two more days passed before I was cleared to travel. Physically, I was fine, still tired, but I'd successfully moved from broth to real food. There was no reason for me not to go home.

Sebastian was, thankfully, correct about Alex's body being able to pass through to Courso as long as it was in contact with his essence. We received word a few hours after they left that the trip across the dimensional boundary was successful. I felt better knowing that the first obstacle was cleared, but was still uncomfortable about leaving. Even though there was nothing rational about it, I felt going back to Arizona would take me farther away from Alex. Of course, that was complete bullshit; now that he was in another dimension, he might as well be on another planet.

Aiden and Cortez were amiable travel companions as we made our way back to Arizona. Now that we didn't have to avoid detection, we used commercial aircraft for the trip. Having to wait for connections made the journey a bit longer than when we flew *Xyzok-Air*, but whoever made the travel arrangements was nice enough to book every leg in first class.

Cortez, as usual, had little to say and spent most of the time either playing video games on his phone or glaring at the other passengers. Aiden was more interactive—and considerably less intimidating—but seemed to understand that I wasn't in the mood for unnecessary conversation. He kept the banter to a minimum.

We took a limo to my place from the airport, and the boys sat like bookends on either side of me in the back seat. Now that I was back on my own turf, and with Otto in custody, it seemed kind of ridiculous to have bodyguards.

"Did you guys escort me because you were on your way back here anyway, or did you draw the short straw to be my babysitters?"

They both seemed perplexed by my question, but I was surprised when Cortez was the one to answer.

"Alex thought you would be more comfortable traveling with someone you had met before, but Aiden and I volunteered. Not as your babysitters—we consider it an honor."

I looked from Aiden back to Cortez. "An honor?"

Aiden nodded. "Certainly. We consider your actions to be courageous. And, if you don't mind my asking, have you had prior defensive training? It's amazing that you had the presence of mind to utilize chopsticks as weaponry."

I winced when he brought up my gruesome use of the eating utensils. The "what the fuck" expression on Angelica's face just before she collapsed wasn't something I was going to forget any time soon. Perhaps never if Alex remained permanently inside her body.

"When she pushed me onto the desk and I saw the chopsticks, I remembered joking with my friends about using something similar to ward off a mugger. I was terrified and just reacted. I didn't mean to kill her; it was pure luck I got her in the eye."

"Luck or skill, if you hadn't killed her, she would have killed you," Cortez offered with a shrug. "And, her death made it possible for Alex to survive. I doubt Angelica would have lost any sleep had you been the one who died."

He was right, of course. The benefit of being completely without moral responsibility or social conscience is you never feel bad about doing horrible things to people. Not being a sociopath, I couldn't ignore the consequences of my actions. Maybe I didn't really want to, because that's what separated me from the likes of Angelica and Otto. Ah yes, overwhelming guilt, the reward for being a good person. My mother would be so proud.

The limo dropped me at the guesthouse and Aiden and Cortez continued on to wherever it was they were going. I dropped my bag near the front door and fished out my phone, which had been returned after our rescue. I hadn't been able to use it when we were outside of the U.S.—my plan didn't cover overseas travel—and was surprised when I turned it on and had a bunch of voicemails. In no mood to listen to them, I speed-dialed Rachel, hoping either she or Harrison were home so I could pick up Vinnie.

Rachel wasn't there, but Harrison was. I told him I'd be right over, and when I arrived, Vinnie was already ensconced in his carrier, howling bloody murder. I worried that, despite Sebastian's absence, my finicky feline might still find me vaguely repellant. My fears were, mercifully, unfounded. When I placed my hand against the metal door grate, Vinnie stopped caterwauling, rubbed his head against my fingers, and purred.

"Thanks so much for taking care of him. I really appreciate it," I said as Harrison walked me out to the car.

"No problem. He was a perfect house guest." Harrison placed a bag with the rest of Vinnie's stuff in the front seat while I buckled the carrier in the back. "I think

Rachel tried to call you a couple of times but couldn't reach you."

"Oh yeah, my phone must have been messed up or something. I just realized I had missed calls today. There wasn't a problem at work, was there?"

Harrison shrugged. "I don't think so; I just thought I'd mention it. Rachel was concerned that you didn't call her back because you were mad at her."

I was about to ask for more details, when Rachel pulled into the driveway. She jumped out of the car and hugged the stuffing out of me.

"Oh my god, Hailey, I'm so happy to see you!" She pulled back from the embrace and looked me over carefully. "Is everything okay? I was worried," she said with a slight frown.

"Everything's fine." I glanced questioningly between Harrison and Rachel. "Why did you think something was wrong?"

"Well, it's weird for you not to call me back when I leave a message, and I texted you a couple of times, too. I just figured you were busy until your mother called at work because she couldn't get in touch with you, either."

Shit. That was the problem with lying, it's almost impossible to tie up every single loose end. No one could have foreseen my mother calling work; she never, ever called me there. I didn't think she even had the number.

I gave myself a hard, mental slap in the head. *Damn it, why didn't I just tell Rachel that my sister didn't want my mother to know about her pregnancy problems, and we were keeping it a secret from her?* "Did you tell her I was at Sarah's?"

"No, it was obvious she had no clue about your sister's pregnancy, so I told her you went on a camping trip and probably didn't have cell phone coverage. I think she bought the story, but the more I thought about it, the more it seemed odd that you would up and leave to go take care of your sister."

She had her hands on her hips and I could tell she was waiting for me to fess up. When I didn't right away, she said, "Does this have anything to do with Alex?"

I hated lying, but couldn't tell her everything. Still, she deserved as much of the truth as I was able to give.

"Yeah, I took some time off to spend with him."

"So why didn't you just say that to begin with?"

"I don't know. I guess I wasn't really sure what was going on between us, and I just met him."

Rachel rolled her eyes.

"Did you worry I'd think you're a slut? For god's sake, Alex seems like a great guy, and you haven't been with anyone for three years. Even if all you wanted was to go somewhere and bang his brains out, do you think I'd think less of you?"

She looked so indignant. I wished I could tell her everything, and not just to assuage my guilt. In the last month or so, I was inhabited by a guy from another dimension, almost murdered by psychos trying to discover the secret to immortality, and ended up killing one of them. The only part that I could share—that I had met an extraordinary guy who made me want to feel again—was tempered by the real possibility that I might never see him again.

Tears started to well up, and I stammered, "I'm really sorry I didn't tell you the truth." I *was* sorry, even though I continued to lie. I hoped my mother was wrong about the underworld being real. With all the lying and killing in the last few days, if it was, there was surely a bonfire down there with my name on it.

She hugged me again. "Hey, I understand." When she pulled away, she wagged her brows and said, "So, was it fantastic?"

I looked into her face, so expectant for even a tidbit of the salacious details. Too bad I didn't have any. What could I say? She already thought I was hopeless in the post-divorce romance department. If I admitted we never actually did the deed after I had just told her I went away with him, I might never hear the end of it.

What the hell, I was probably already going there, one more fib wouldn't make much difference. I wiped the tears from my eyes and said as convincingly as I could, "It was fantastic."

"So, is he back in Portland? When are you going to see him again?"

"I don't know. It's ... it's complicated."

"That's not good," Harrison offered, shaking his head.

"I just need some time to sort things out." They both looked kind of concerned, so I forced myself to smile. "Don't worry; I'll be fine, I promise. I just need to get home and get some sleep right now. I'll see you at work tomorrow, Rach."

Exhausted from the long trip, I climbed into my car and managed to drive home without either falling asleep at the wheel or crying like a baby. Vinnie was thrilled to be in familiar territory—when I set the carrier down in the living room and opened the door, he shot out and ran around the place a couple of times before coming back to weave his body around my ankles. I gathered him in my arms and sat down on the sofa, and he proceeded to curl up in my lap.

It was nice being back. It also felt odd to be alone. I hadn't realized how used to Sebastian's essence I had become. Even when he wasn't talking in my head, there was always a kind of energy associated with his presence. So much had happened in the last couple of days I hadn't noticed his absence.

I missed Sebastian, but I really missed Alex. Since my divorce, I thought I was comfortable being by myself most of the time. Whatever the reason for my sudden revelation, I didn't just feel alone. I was lonely. And that made me very sad.

I went back to work the next day, but my heart wasn't really in it. It was nice to see Chelsea, Daniel, and the critters, but I plodded robotically through my duties. It wasn't just melancholy from worrying about Alex. After everything that had happened, it didn't feel right going back to my old life. It was tough dealing with the fact that I killed someone. Sure, rationally I knew it was her or me, but it wasn't something I could just gloss over. Also, now that I knew there was—literally—a whole other world out there, supervising a chinchilla-milking facility just didn't seem like a productive way to earn a living.

So, two weeks after I got back, I gave notice. I probably should have stuck it out until I found another job, but I had no idea what I wanted to do. Besides, what's the point of having savings if you can't use it to indulge yourself? My car was paid for, rent was cheap, and I figured I had a good year or so to figure it all out before I would be forced to find gainful employment. *Yay, me.*

Rachel, Chelsea, and Daniel organized a going away party at O'Reilly's after my last day. It was bittersweet, but it wasn't like I'd never see them again. I would be seeing less of them, but they'd always be a part of my life, whatever that turned out to be.

Once free from the daily routine of going into work, I spent a lot of time thinking. I still had no word about, or from, Alex. I knew he couldn't pick up a phone or email, but as time went on my previously ingrained mindset— that I was not meant for happily-ever-after—started to overtake my more recently developed sense of hopefulness. I tried to remain positive, but had no idea how Alex really felt about me before, much less how any of the monumental changes that had recently occurred might influence him now.

I did come to one important conclusion. One night about a week after my last day at work, I sat outside looking up at the full moon, recalling Alex's handsome face, bathed in the glow of the moonlight. I've always considered myself completely heterosexual, and at first, I couldn't even imagine being sexually attracted to Alex as a woman. The more I thought about it, the more I realized that I loved Alex regardless of his physical form. I also realized that any hesitation on my part was not because he was in a woman's body, it was because of the woman's body he was in. I didn't know if I would ever be able to look at that face without reliving what it felt like to spear her, or how Angelica looked when she died.

I also knew that while I still clung to the hope that I would see him again, even if I didn't, I didn't regret loving him. If he did come back still inside Angelica, and he still wanted me, we could figure it all out together.

~20~

One of the best things about not having to go to work every day was being able to take hikes in the morning whenever the feeling struck. Now that it was almost April, the desert was awakening from winter into spring, and I was anxious to check out the wildflowers. The display varied from year to year depending on the amount of rain in the fall, and, luckily, we had enough precipitation when it counted to foster a decent show. I chose the Fifty-Year Trail on the north side of the Santa Catalina range, and it didn't disappoint.

It had rained a bit the night before, and there was nothing as wonderful as the smell of the desert afterward. It's difficult to describe the unique scent, but it was earthy, fresh, and heavenly. The hillsides along the trail were blanketed in color: low growing Mexican gold poppies mixed with tall, bright pink penstemon, huge white desert chicory, and spiky lavender lupine. I even found some mountain larkspur interspersed among the flowers. The bright blue petals reminded me of Alex's eyes.

The landscape was breathtaking and peaceful, and the hike rejuvenated me. By the time I got home, showered, and had lunch, it was well after one o'clock. I was getting ready to go outside to tend my newly planted tomato garden—I needed to put up a barrier to keep both the birds and rabbits from devouring the fruit once it ripened—when the doorbell rang.

I wasn't expecting anyone and debated not answering, but the bell rang again. Anyone that persistent should probably not be completely ignored.

"Whatever it is, I'm not interested," I barked through the closed door.

"Okay, but I'm not selling anything," replied a familiar baritone.

I flung open the door and there he was—tall, blond, and handsome, sporting a hesitant smile on his face and a single, white rose in his hand.

"Alex!" I shouted, launching myself into him, my unbridled enthusiasm forcing the flower from his hand.

He wrapped me in his arms and held me tight. My head was kind of smashed into his chest, but I managed to murmur, "I missed you," into his shirt.

"I missed you too." Alex began to trail kisses from the top of my head down the side of my cheek. When his lips finally reached mine, the soft kisses became more fervent and heated. Without breaking the contact, he lifted me off my feet and moved us inside, kicking the door closed with his foot.

We continued this way for a while longer until I pulled back to really look at him.

"You're ... you again," was all I could say.

"I am, but it was more difficult than anticipated."

"Tell me everything." I pulled him over to the sofa and we sat, fingers laced together, as I waited expectantly for the details.

"My corporeal-self was resistant to healing, partly because my spiritual-self was no longer directly linked to it, but also because of the extensive damage caused by the bullets. Eventually, the master healers were able to repair everything, except for my heart. They believed that it wouldn't withstand the stress of reconvergence and Sebastian was concerned yanking my essence from my dying body a second time might not be wise. They strongly suggested that I remain in Angelica."

Alex paused and glanced out the window. "I realized one's essence is aligned with their body, and you can't just randomly interchange parts."

He looked back at me. "I don't know, maybe after a while things would have adjusted, but I really just wanted me. Besides, the whole process defies the natural order, so we embarked on an alternative plan. Sebastian deconverged me from Angelica's body into his laptop, as he had originally hoped to do with himself before he ended up in your Kindle. He postulated that a controlled transfer to a healthy body would pose less risk. Then, Angelica's heart was removed and placed in me. When they knew the transplant was successful, Sebastian successfully reconverged my spiritual essence."

"Wow. First vampires, werewolves, and ghosts, now Frankenstein," I joked.

Alex lifted an eyebrow. "Well, that's one way to look at it, I suppose. Except I'm missing the neck hardware."

"Good thing. I'm not really a neck-bolt kind of a gal."

I looked him up and down carefully, trying to see if anything seemed different, but he seemed exactly the same as he had before.

"How do you feel?"

"I feel great. I'm sorry you were left in the dark all this time. I wanted to send someone to give you updates, but Sebastian was so unsure if any of this would work, he convinced me that it might be best to wait until things were resolved one way or the other."

I knew they were trying to make things easier for me, but really, why would anyone think I'd prefer ignorance rather than deal with what was actually going on? The scenarios conjured up in my mind were a lot more stressful than reality. The truth you can deal with, it's all the speculative crap that makes you nuts. Now wasn't the time to quibble over what would have been a better choice. Alex was alive and well, and that was all that mattered.

When I didn't respond, Alex reached over and stroked my hair.

"I was worried what happened in the castle and everything after might be too much and you would choose to discontinue our relationship."

"You can't get rid of me that easily, Blondie," I whispered, leaning in to press my lips to his. He started to say something, but I shushed him. "Shut up. We can talk later."

As he scooped me in his arms and lifted me from the sofa, I was already unbuttoning his shirt. By the time he deposited me on the bed, I was able to run my hands across the muscular planes of his bare chest. Looming over me, he removed his shirt, and helped relieve me of mine. I hadn't bothered with a bra—another bonus of unemployment—and he gazed appreciatively before leaning down to kiss me. There was nothing hesitant about him now; our tongues danced against each other's as he stroked my breasts with one hand, deftly undoing my jeans with the other.

I groaned with annoyance when he stopped, but rethought my objection when he unzipped his pants and pulled them off. In all the time we spent together in New Hampshire, I had never actually seen him this undressed, and had wondered if he was a brief or boxer guy. Apparently, he was neither. What was revealed when those pants cleared his hips was just as I had imagined, and it still made my breath catch in my throat.

I considered that three years without sex might have skewed my assessment ability, but he seemed really well endowed. Of course, it's not like I had a lot to compare him to; maybe the four other guys I'd slept with were phallus-light.

I resolved to concentrate on the business at hand, and I did just that to Alex. Not surprisingly, he felt as good as he looked. His eyes closed and his breath became more ragged as I stroked his length. Alex moved away from me slightly, to allow the removal of my jeans and thong— thankfully, I hadn't put on granny panties—and then focused his masterful mouth on my breasts.

I grabbed his head and ran my fingers through his hair as he concentrated first on one nipple, then the other. Just when I thought nothing could be more adept than his tongue, his hand slipped between my legs and the skillful use of his fingers proved me wrong. Intense pleasure rocketed through me and I propelled my hips against him, crying out when I finally climaxed a few moments later.

I lay there, boneless and reveling in aftershocks. When Alex began kissing me again, I was too out of it to react much beyond an occasional, satisfied moan. When I finally regrouped mentally, at least somewhat, I was feeling a little guilty that Alex had done all the work while I had reaped all the rewards. I also became coherent enough to remember that for things to progress, birth control measures were required.

"Ah, Alex?" It was still difficult to form complete sentences and he didn't make it any easier with his mouth clamped over mine. "I hate to bring this up, but before we go any further ..."

"Hmmm?" he murmured against my lips.

I shifted a little to avoid his tongue long enough to complete my thought.

"Condom?"

He looked down at me, realization flashing across his previously passion-filled face.

"I didn't bring any," he replied after an extended pause.

"Top drawer of my nightstand."

He paused again, and for a moment I thought he had something to say. Instead, he sat up, turned his back to me and opened the drawer.

"Hailey," he said, his voice hesitant, "why do you have a basket filled with condoms next to your bed?"

"For my last birthday, Rachel and Chelsea thought it would be hilarious to buy me fancy condoms. They considered it ironic since the chances of my using them were so slim."

I could see his shoulders move up and down, trying to suppress his laughter.

"Well, they certainly assembled quite an assortment," he said, finally. "I had no idea there was such a wide variety."

He then reached in and grabbed one. I heard a wrapper tear and could tell he was rolling it on, by both the sound it made, and the movement of his arms from behind. Alex looked over his shoulder and flashed a wicked smile my way. Then he stood and turned around.

The condom he had chosen was tricolored—blue on the bottom, white in the middle and red on top—and it even had a rounded point at the end. It looked just like a Rocket Pop.

"You think it's flavored?" I asked.

He started to turn back to check the wrapper, but I did my own investigation, sliding my tongue up the entire length and back down the other side. In the interest of data collection, I repeated the test a couple of times before I was certain. This time, it was more than my breath that was caught in my throat.

"Definitely not flavored," I declared once I'd completed the investigation.

Alex flipped me onto my back and hovered over me. "Then let's not waste it on your taste buds."

I wrapped my legs around him and he entered me, slowly, until I had taken him in completely. He kissed me, and asked in a raspy voice, "You okay?"

I was way more than okay. It felt fantastic, but instead of wasting time answering, I began moving against him to show just how okay I was. We synchronized our movements, slowly at first, then building in rhythmic intensity. This time when I came, we did it together. That's also how it happened when we made love a second time, except it was at night, so we used a glow-in-the-dark condom instead.

The next morning, I awoke curled around Alex, with Vinnie sleeping on my pillow next to my head. I ignored the cat and nuzzled Alex's neck until he rolled onto his back and pressed my head against his chest.

He kissed the top of my head and said groggily, "I really enjoyed sleeping with you before, but I've got to say, this is much, much better."

I snuggled in closer. "Yeah, waking up satisfied is way better than waking up frustrated."

Alex glanced over at the clock radio on the nightstand. "Hailey, it's after eight, aren't you going to be late for work?"

"I quit," I mumbled into his collarbone.

"Really? When? Why?"

I propped myself up on one elbow. "Shortly after I got back. I want to do something more … I don't know … more socially redeeming."

Alex shifted onto his side and stroked my cheek. "Well, I always thought you were capable of a lot more."

"Yeah, Sebastian said the same thing."

"He did, did he?"

"Well, I believe he said something closer to, 'My dear, you are wasting yourself milking rodents so people with more money than sense can indulge their feckless, ethically bankrupt lifestyles with useless consumerism'."

"That sounds more like Sebastian," Alex said, grinning. "Have any ideas what you might want to do instead of encouraging rich people's extravagant food choices?"

I shrugged. "Not a clue."

Running my hand idly over his rippled abs, I realized that if he had a heart transplant, there should be one big-ass scar on his chest. All I felt were the same angled ones he'd had before.

"How come you don't have a scar here?" I asked, trailing a finger down his sternum. "You have all these others."

"Remember in New Hampshire when you got burned and there was no scar after I healed it? The transplant scar was healed in the same way. I've chosen to keep the marks from wounds I received when I was forced to dispatch someone who refused to be apprehended. That way, I can never forget. Not that I dwell on those I've killed while performing my *Xyzok* duties, but even when there is no other alternative, taking a life should never be taken lightly."

I flopped over on my back and stared up at the ceiling. "I don't think I'll ever forget how it felt to kill Angelica," I said softly.

Alex pulled me to him and draped his arm over me. "I'm sorry you had to experience that, but I'm not sorry Angelica was the one to die instead of you. I should have realized that you might be troubled by it, and regret that I didn't arrange to have a someone from Courso help you work through it while I was gone."

"Hey, it's okay. You had enough on your mind." I looked again at the faded marks crisscrossing his flesh.

"I'm here now, and I'll help you deal with what you were forced to do." He kissed me softly. "Some scars are best left on the outside."

~21~

After two days of pretty much nothing but making love, eating, and sleeping, Alex and I finally put some clothes on. That's kind of an exaggeration; we put some clothes on when we went to the kitchen for food, but somehow, they never stayed on for very long. We did take a few showers during the forty-eight hours of erotic bliss, but we had ended up messing around then, too, so to be fair, I had to count that under the heading of "making love." Actually, the only reason we came up for air when we did was because we had exhausted the gift basket-supply of protection and had to make a trip to the drugstore.

On the drive back, Alex and I discussed possible jobs I might find interesting. The problem was, many of the things I might like to do, I wasn't really qualified for, or would require a butt load of additional classes. I vowed to never study for or take tests again, because every so often, even years after finishing my master's degree, I'd dream it was the end of the semester, and had registered for a class, but never went to it. I was completely screwed because it was too late to drop and there was no way to make up all the work I had missed.

"You know, you could work for me," Alex offered.

"Well, I'm sure the fringe benefits would be fantastic."

"No, I'm serious. You're smart, you have more common sense than most people I know—human or Courso—and you have an inquisitive mind that cuts through the bullshit and focuses in on what's important. You would be a big help with research and low-level field work."

"Low-level?"

"I mean nothing dangerous. However, there are things that humans are better suited for, particularly when it comes to surveillance. Courso criminals tend to overlook humans because they think, and usually rightly so, that they are no threat."

I let out a derisive harrumph. "Yeah, that's just what Otto and Angelica thought, and look what happened to them."

Alex smiled. "My point exactly."

It was an intriguing idea. But my previous foray into *Xyzok* business hadn't really ended all that well.

"I don't know, Alex. I'll have to think about it."

"No pressure," Alex said with a shrug. "Just throwing it out there as a possibility, but I think you'd be a natural."

***

Everything was going so well, I should have known it was too good to be true. A couple of days later, while pinning Vinnie to the floor during a mostly unsuccessful attempt to trim his razor-sharp nails, the song, *She Drives Me Crazy* blared from my phone. *Great, my mother.*

I had no problem blowing her off, and continued with Vinnie's pedicure. Unfortunately, Alex didn't remember that was my mother's unique ring tone. Knowing I was occupied, he answered in my stead.

From the other room, I heard, "Hello." Pause. "No, you don't have the wrong number. This is Hailey's phone." Pause. "Just a minute, I'll get her."

I sighed, knowing there was no way to avoid the conversation. I made a mental note to make certain Alex knew to never, ever tell my mother I was home without asking me first.

I let the cat go—at least he had reason to be happy my mother called—and took the phone from Alex. He noticed my exasperated expression; it would have been hard for him not to. I might as well have had a sign on my head that said, "Caution. Extremely Annoyed Woman."

He looked so crestfallen. I waved him off and mouthed, "It's okay."

With as much perkiness as I could muster, I chirped, "Hi Mom."

"Hailey, it is not even eight o'clock in the morning. Who is that man that answered your phone?" she barked out, not bothering with normal pleasantries like "Hello" or "How are you?" much less her usual and completely unnecessary, "It's your mother."

"That's Alex," I explained. "I was busy, so he answered for me."

"And why is he there so early?"

"Mom, really." I could see where this was going, and it wasn't going to be pretty.

"Don't you use that tone with me, young lady. I am your mother, and I deserve an answer to my question."

"Mom, I am not a child. I'm thirty years old and have lived on my own since I went off to college. I don't think I need to justify who is in my house and when."

"Oh, my dear lord! Did he spend the night with you? What nice man will ever want you now that you have been despoiled?"

Despoiled? Had she really just said that?

"In case you've forgotten, I'm not a virgin. I was married, remember?"

I could hear her mumbling under her breath, and I knew the waterworks were going to start any time now.

"Hailey Parrish. You know very well that I formed a prayer circle after your divorce and the Lord spoke to me and said your purity had been restored. But now ..." Her voice trailed off into a muffled sob.

My head started to pound, and I knew my blood pressure was rising. I should have ended the call then, but said, "Look, I wasn't exactly a virgin before I got married, so it's all kind of a moot point."

I knew it was ill-advised to bait her like that. With little patience for her histrionics in the best of times, given all that had transpired lately, my ability to deal with her was at an all-time low. Still, the way she was wailing and carrying on, you'd have thought I told her I had taken up Satanism.

"Mom," I said gently, tempering my tone to mask my annoyance.

"Where did I go wrong? Where did I go wrong?"

"Mom!" This time I shouted. "Look, I'm sorry you're upset, but I'm not having this argument with you right now. I'm not despoiled and I'm not some harlot who needs saving. Say hi to Dad. I'll talk to you some other time."

I disconnected, flung the phone onto the sofa, and let out a long, loud, frustrated scream. "That woman drives me insane!"

"Ah," Alex noted. "That explains the ring tone."

Stomping to the patio door, I intended to open the vertical blinds to go outside for some fresh air. I was so agitated, however, I kept pulling the wrong cord. Instead of the slats moving together and sliding out of the way to allow access to the door, they just rotated. My already off the chart anxiety level ratcheted skyward, and I spun around, thinking about how good it would feel to break something.

As the thought materialized in my head, a warm sensation tingled through my fingers. The prickles soon morphed into a rush of energy, my hands shot out in front of me, and the kitchen table splintered.

Vinnie darted away from the pieces of wood flying in all directions, hissed, and ran from the room. Similarly shocked by the carnage, I gawked at what remained of the table, then at my hands, which were still extended. I could swear there were tiny puffs of smoke rising from them.

Horrified and befuddled, I shifted my gaze to Alex. Surprisingly, he seemed a lot less shocked than I'd expected, given that I just annihilated a piece of solid oak furniture. Instead of eyeing me with the same incredulous disgust I felt for myself, he blinked, calmly pulled his phone from his pocket, and punched in a number.

A moment later, looking directly at me as he spoke, he said, "Sebastian? It's Alex. I think we have a problem."

~The End~

Thank you for reading *Special Offers*. Feedback is crucial for any author to succeed. Please take a moment to leave a review. Even a few words can help future readers make an informed decision about purchasing my work.

ABOUT THE AUTHOR

M.L. Ryan is a professional woman – which is not to say that she gave up her amateur status, but rather that she is over-educated with a job that reflects her one-time reluctance to leave school and get "real" work – and she spends a lot of time in that profession reading highly technical material. She has many stories rolling around in her head, and she finally decided to write some of them. She prefers literature that isn't saddled with excruciating symbolism, ponderous dialogue or worldly implications. She also doesn't like plots so reliant on love at first sight— they give her migraines.

M.L. lives in Tucson, Arizona with her husband and teenage son, three cats, two Curly-coated retrievers, and an adopted desert tortoise.

****

More of the Coursodon Dimension series, available in paperback on Amazon, CreateSpace and Barnes and Noble:

Special Rewards
Special Attraction
Special Passage
Special Deceptions
Special Conceptions

Contact M.L. Ryan at: www.coursodondimension.com

On Facebook: http://www.facebook.com/pages/ML-Ryan/206558312774847

Twitter: @MLRyan1